THE SWORDSMAN OF MARS

THE SWORDSMAN OF MARS

OF MARS

by Otis Adelbert Kline

PROLOGUE

Harry Thorne opened his eyes and gazed about him with a startled expression. This was not the tawdry hotel bedroom in which he had gone to sleep; it was a small room with bare, concrete walls, a door of hardwood planking studded with bolts, and a barred window. The only articles of furniture were the cot on which he was lying, a chair, and a small table.

So the sleeping pills didn't finish me off, he thought. *Now I'm in jail for attempted suicide!*

Thorne sat up, then rose unsteadily to his feet and staggered to the window. Supporting himself by gripping the thick iron bars, he peered out. It was broad daylight and the sun was high in the heavens. Below him stretched a deep valley, through which a narrow stream meandered. And as far as he could see in all directions there were mountains, though the highest peaks were all below the level of his own eyes.

He turned from the window at the sound of a key grating in a lock. Then the heavy door swung inward, and a large man entered the cell, bearing a tray of food and a steaming pot of coffee. Behind the man was a still larger figure, whose very presence radiated authority. His forehead was high and bulged outward over shaggy eyebrows that met above his aquiline nose. He wore a pointed, closely cropped Vandyke, black with a slight sprinkling of gray, and was dressed in faultlessly tailored evening clothes.

Thorne got to his feet as his singular visitor closed the door behind him. Then, in a booming bass, the man said, "At last, Mr. Thorne, I have caught up with you. I am Dr. Morgan." He smiled. "And, I might add, not a moment too soon. You gave us quite a time—Boyd and I managed to get you out of that hotel room and down to the street, passing you off as drunk. Don't you remember a knocking at the door? You weren't quite out when we came in."

Thorne thought for a moment, then nodded. It seemed that there had been a pounding somewhere. "How did you get in? I thought I locked the door."

"You did—but I had skeleton keys with me, just in case. We took you to my apartment, treated you, and brought you out here." Morgan nodded to Boyd, who left the room, then waved his hand invitingly toward the tray. "I ordered breakfast served in your room. I especially urge you to try the coffee. It will counteract the effect of the sedatives I was compelled to use in order to save your life and bring you here."

5

"You've gone to a lot of trouble to save something I don't want," Thorne said. "May I ask why you are interfering in my affairs?"

"I need you," Morgan replied simply. "And I can offer you adventure such as only one other man of Earth has known—possibly glory, possibly death. But if death, not the mean sort you were seeking."

Harry Thorne frowned. "You referred to a man of Earth as if there were men not of Earth. Are you suggesting a trip to Mars?"

Dr. Morgan laughed. "Splendid, Mr. Thorne. But suppose you tackle this breakfast. It will put you in a better frame of mind for what I am going to tell you. I shall not lock the door as I leave. When you have finished, join me in the drawing room—at the end of the corridor to your right." He paused in the doorway. "You mentioned a trip to Mars, Mr. Thorne. Forgive me if I keep you in suspense for a time, but—although it is not exactly what you think those words mean—that is what I am going to propose."

CHAPTER 1

"You have heard of telepathy, of course—in fact, Mr. Thorne, you experimented with it at one time."

"How did you know that, doctor?"

"You wrote a letter about your experiments to the editor of a popular magazine. It was published under your own name two months ago."

Thorne rubbed his brow. "That's right, I did—been so busy I forgot all about it. But my results were negative."

Dr. Morgan nodded. "So were mine, for nearly twenty years. It was a hobby when I was in practice, but since my retirement, I've devoted my full time to it. Let me brief you on the basics.

"Telepathy, the communication of thoughts or ideas from one mind to another without the use of any physical medium whatever, is not influenced or hampered by either time or space. That is fundamental, but I had to amend it. I failed to achieve anything until I succeeded in building a device which would pick up and amplify thought waves. And even then I would have failed had this machine not caught the waves projected by another machine which another man had built to amplify and project them."

"You mean you can read minds by radio, as it were?" Thorne asked.

"To a very limited extent. If you had a projector in this room, and I had my receiver here, I could pick up any thoughts you sent me—but only those you consciously projected. I could not read your mind in the sense of picking up anything you did not want me to know."

Thorne took a cigarette from the box on the table to his right and lit it. "Interesting," he admitted, "but what has this to do with Mars?"

"I made only one amendment to that basic theory, Mr. Thorne. The rest of it holds true: the communication of thoughts or ideas from one mind to another is not influenced or hampered by time or space. The man who built the thought-projector is on Mars."

"Men on Mars—you mean Martians, or human beings like us? Excuse me, doctor, but that is spreading it a bit thick. I'm well enough up on present-day studies of the planets . . ."

". . . to know that the existence of a human civilization on Mars today is hardly credible," Morgan broke in. "You are quite right. None such exists."

"Then how . . .?"

"Space or *time*. I was incredulous, too, when I got in touch with someone who identified himself as a human being, one Lal Vak, a Martian scientist and psychologist. And I might add that Lal Vak found the idea of a human civilization on Earth a bit thick, too. But the explanation, fantastic as it may seem, is quite simple: Lal Vak is speaking to me from the Mars of some millions of years ago, when a human civilization *did* exist there."

Morgan raised his hand. "Don't interrupt now—hear me out. From that simple exchange of visual and auditory impressions which marked our first communications, we progressed until each one had learned the language of the other to a degree that enabled us to exchange abstract as well as concrete ideas.

"It was Lal Vak who suggested that if we could find a man on Earth and one on Mars whose bodies were similar enough to be doubles, their brain patterns might also be similar enough so that consciousness could be transferred between them. Thus, Earth of the 20th Century could be viewed through Martian eyes, while the (to us) ancient Mars culture—we cannot yet place it in time relative to Earth—could be seen at first hand by a man from Earth. First Lal Vak projected to me many thought images of Martians willing to make this exchange—so clearly that I was able to draw detailed pictures of them. But that was not enough. I could spend the rest of my life without finding any counterparts of these Martians here. The second

7

thing Lal Vak did was to tell me how to make what we call a mind-compass, and gave me the brain-patterns of his volunteers. I followed his directions and fed the first brain-pattern into the mind-compass."

Thorne leaned forward intently. "What happened?"

"Nothing. The needle rotated aimlessly. This meant that either there was no physical counterpart of this Martian now alive on earth, or any such double did not have a similar brain-pattern. I fed in the second and third patterns with the same result. But with the fourth pattern, the needle swung directly to a given point and remained there." Morgan opened a drawer in the little table and took out some pencil sketches. "Recognize this man?" he asked, handing a sketch to Thorne.

"Your assistant—Boyd, you called him?"

"Correct. Under the influence of Lal Vak's thoughts, I drew a picture of Frank Boyd. To shorten the story, I found him in an Alaskan mining camp. He was interested in the venture I proposed—he is now on Mars."

"But—I just saw him . . ."

"You saw the body of Frank Boyd, which is now inhabited by Sel Han, a Martian. On Mars, Sel Han's body is occupied by Frank Boyd, an Earthman. But I made one terrible mistake."

"What was that?"

"In my eagerness to find a volunteer, I did not investigate Frank Boyd. Sel Han has cooperated with Lal Vak and me, but once on Mars, Frank Boyd broke contact—and without his cooperation, it could not be maintained. I have learned through Lal Vak that Boyd has allied himself with a group of Martians who are out to seize power and set up an empire over the entire planet. Mars is presently in a state roughly analogous to our middle ages, socially, though in some branches of science they are in advance of us. But theirs is not a machine civilization, and an adventurer who is also a fighting man—or adept at intrigue—can go far there."

Harry Thorne grinned. "Let me see if I can guess the rest of the story. You've loosed an unsavory character on Mars and feel you've wronged your friend, Lal Vak, so you want to undo the damage if you can. You fed more brain-patterns into the object compass, and eventually the brain-pattern of . . ."

". . . This man," Morgan agreed, passing him another sketch. Thorne took it and saw a drawing of himself in minute detail.

"But that was not enough," he said. "You didn't want to repeat your error, so you spent some time investigating me first."

Dr. Morgan smiled. "And the results were most satisfactory—to me. You had a good war record in Korea, you've been on hunting expeditions to Africa, and you've been in business. Your recent difficulties, which resulted in the loss of your fiancée and your business—left you a pauper, in fact—came out of your refusal to go along with your partner's dubious (though legal) manipulations. He wiped you out and took your girl, too. . . . In short, you are a man who might well do what Lal Vak and I feared impossible."

Harry Thorne nodded. "Assuming that you can send me on this strange mission, what would you want me to do?"

"Only two things. Remain in touch with me, through Lal Vak, as much as possible, and, if you can, kill Frank Boyd—the Martian Sel Han. Otherwise, your life on Mars will be your own, to live as you choose, or as the Martians choose to let you live. If you are able to rise above your environment—as I think you will be—you will find opportunities there you could never hope for here. You will find a world of romance and adventure undreamed of outside of fiction. And if you are not equally quick with sword and wits, you will find death. Knowing you to be an expert fencer—yes, I found out that you had tried to get a job with a fencing instructor and was turned down because you beat him too easily—I don't think I need worry about you on the first count."

"The prospect appeals to me," Thorne admitted. "But I refuse to murder a man I have never seen."

"If you oppose Sel Han's designs, I assure you that you will have to kill him or be killed. There's no question of murder—it will be simple and justifiable self-defense. . . . Then—you'll go?"

"I'll at least make the attempt, with your assistance. How does this personality-transfer take place?"

"I can only describe it as a sort of phasing of similar vibrations, represented by your brain-pattern and that of the Martian volunteer. But first I must put you under hypnosis. Then I will contact Lal Vak, and we will work together. He will be on hand to meet you when you awake in the body of a Martian. Now come over here and lie on the sofa."

Thorne did as Dr. Morgan directed, and found that he was looking into a mirror painted with alternate circles of red and black. The doctor touched a button and the mirror began to rotate slowly. Morgan's voice came to him, "Now think of that distant world, far off in time and space. Think of it beckoning you."

Thorne obeyed, his eyes fixed on the mirror. He began to feel drowsy, a pleasant lassitude stealing over him. The doctor's voice faded. . . .

CHAPTER 2

Thorne opened his eyes and looked up into a cloudless blue-gray sky that was like a vault of burnished steel. A diminutive sun blazed down upon him but oddly enough, with its heat and light seemingly unimpaired.

The heat, in fact, was so great that it made him draw back into the relatively cold shade of the scaly-trunked conifer that towered above him, its crown of needle-like foliage gathered into a bellshaped tuft. Then conviction came to him. He was really on Mars! Wide awake, now, he sat bolt upright and looked about him. The tree that sheltered him stood alone in a small depression, surrounded by a billowing sea of ochre-yellow sand.

He scrambled to his feet, and as he did so, something clanked at his side. Two straight-bladed weapons hung there, both sheathed in a gray metal that resembled aluminum. One, he judged, was a Martian dagger, and the other a sword. The hilt of the larger weapon was fashioned of a metal of the color of brass, the pommel representing a serpent's head, the grip, its body, and the guard, the continuation of the body and tail coiled in the form of a figure eight. The hilt of the dagger was like that of the sword, but smaller.

Thorne drew the sword from its sheath. The steel blade was slender and two-edged, and tapered to a needlelike point. Both edges were armed with tiny razor-sharp teeth which he instantly saw would add greatly to its effectiveness as a cutting weapon. He tested its balance and found he could wield it as easily as any duelling sword he had ever had in his hand.

Replacing the sword in the sheath, he examined the dagger, and found it also edged with tiny teeth. The blade of this weapon was about ten inches in length.

Depending from the belt on the other side, and heavy enough to balance the weight of the sword and dagger, was a mace with a short brazen handle and a disk-shaped head of steel which was fastened fanwise on the haft, thick at the middle and tapering out at the edges to sawlike teeth, much coarser and longer than those on sword or dagger.

Thorne turned his attention to his apparel. He was wearing a breechclout of soft leather. Beneath this, and down to the center of his shins, his limbs were bare and considerably sunburned. Below this point were the rolled tops of a pair of long boots, made from fur and fitted with clasps which were obviously for the purpose of attaching them to the bottom of the breechclout when they were drawn up.

Above the waist his sun-tanned body was bare of clothing, but he wore a pair of broad metal armlets, a pair of bracelets with long bars attached, evidently to protect the forearm from sword cuts, and a jewelled medallion, suspended on his chest from a chain around his neck and inscribed with strange characters.

On his head was a bundle of silky material with a short, soft nap, rolled much like a turban and held in place by one brass-studded strap that passed around his forehead, and another that went beneath his chin.

Beyond a large sand dune, and not more than a quarter of a mile distant, he saw the waving bell-shaped crowns of a small grove of trees similar to the one that sheltered him. He started toward the clump of conifers.

As soon as he stepped out into the blaze of the midday sun, Thorne began to feel uncomfortably warm. Soon he noted other signs of Martian life. Immense, gaudily tinted butterflies, some with wing spreads of more than six feet, flew up from the flower patches at his approach. A huge dragon fly zoomed past, looking much like a miniature airplane.

Suddenly he heard an angry hum beside him, and felt a searing pain in his left side. Seemingly out of nowhere a fly, yellow and red in color and about two feet in length, had darted down upon him and plunged its many-pointed proboscis into his flesh. Seizing the sharp bill of his assailant, he wrenched it from his side.

The insect buzzed violently but Thorne, still clinging to its bill, reached for his dagger with the other hand and cut off its head. Flinging the hideous thing at the body, he caught up a handful of sand to stanch the bleeding of his wound. Presently, he started forward once more.

He was nearing the top of the dune when he saw, coming over the ridge from the other side, a most singular figure. At first glance it looked much like a walking umbrella. Then it resolved itself into a man wearing a long loose-sleeved cloak which covered him from the crown of his head to his knees. Below the cloak the end of a scabbard was visible, as were a pair of rolled fur boots like those worn by Thorne. The face was covered with a mask of flexible transparent material.

Thorne stopped, and instinctively his hand went to his sword hilt.

The other halted, also, at a distance of about ten paces, and swept off his mask. His face was smooth shaven and his hair and eyebrows were white.

11

"I have the honor of being the first man to welcome you to Mars. Harry Thorne," he said in English, and smilingly added: "I am Lal Vak."

Thorne returned his smile. "Thank you, Lal Vak. You speak excellent English."

"I learned your language from Dr. Morgan, just as he learned mine from me. Aural impressions are as readily transmitted by telepathy as visual impressions, you know."

"So the doctor informed me," said Thorne. "But where do we go from here? I'm beginning to feel uncomfortable in this sun."

"I've been inexcusably thoughtless," apologized Lal Vak. "Here, let me show you how to adjust your head-cloak." Reaching up to Thorne's turbanlike headpiece, he loosened a strap. The silky material instantly fell down about the Earthman, reaching to his knees. A flexible, transparent mask also unrolled, and Lal Vak showed him how to draw it across his face.

"This material," he said, "is made from the skin of a large moth. The people of Xancibar, the nation of which you are now a citizen, use these cloaks much for summer wear, particularly when traveling in the desert. They keep out the sun's rays by day, and keep in considerable warmth at night. As you will learn, even our summer nights are quite cold. The mask is made from the same material, but is treated with oil and has the nap scraped off to make it transparent."

"I feel better already," said Thorne. "Now what?"

"Now we will get our mounts, and fly back to the military training school, which you, as Borgen Takkor, must continue to attend. At the school I am an instructor in tactics."

As they approached the small clump of trees which Thorne had previously noticed, he saw that they surrounded a small pool of water. Splashing about in this pool were two immense winged creatures, and Thorne noted with astonishment that they were covered with brown fur instead of feathers. They had long, sturdy legs, covered with yellow scales. Their wings were membranous, and their bills were flat, much like those of ducks, except that they had sharp, down-curved hooks at the end. And when one opened its mouth, Thorne saw that it was furnished with sharp, triangular teeth, tilted backward. These immense beast-birds, whose backs were about seven feet above the ground, and whose heads reached to a height of about twelve feet, were saddled with seats of gray metal.

The tips of each creature's wings were perforated, and tethered to the saddle by means of snap-hooks and short chains, evidently to prevent their taking to the air without their riders.

Lal Vak made a peculiar sound, a low quavering call. Instantly both of the grotesque mounts answered with hoarse honking sounds and came floundering up out of the water toward them. One of them, on coming up to Thorne, arched its neck then lowered its head and nuzzled him violently with its broad bill.

"Scratch his head," said Lal Vak, with an amused smile. "Borgen made quite a pet of him, and you are now Borgen Takkor to him."

After a second prod from the huge beak, Thorne hastily scratched the creature's head, whereupon it held still, blinking contentedly, and making little guttural noises in its throat. He noticed that there was a light strand of twisted leather around its neck, fastened to the end of a flexible rod, which in turn was fastened to the ringshaped pommel of the saddle.

"Is that the steering gear?"

"You have guessed right, my friend," replied Lal Vak. "Pull up on the rod, and the gawr will fly upward. Push down and he will descend. A pull to the right or left and he will fly, walk or swim in the direction indicated according to whether he is in the air, on the ground, or in the water. Pull straight backward, and he will stop or hover."

"Sounds easy."

"It is quite simple. But before we go, let me warn you to speak to no one, whether you are spoken to or not. Salute those who greet you, thus." He raised his left hand to the level of his forehead, with the palm backward. "I must get you to your room as quickly as possible. There you will feign illness, and I will teach you our language before you venture out."

"But how can I remember all the friends and acquaintances of Borg—Borgen Takkor. What a name! Suppose something should come up . . ."

"I've provided against all that. Your illness will be blamed for your temporary loss of memory. This will give you time to find out things, and the right to ask questions rather than answer them. But, come, it grows late. Watch me carefully, and do as I do."

Lal Vak rugged at a folded wing, and his mount knelt. Then he climbed into the saddle and unfastened the snaphooks which tethered the wings, hooking them through two rings in his own belt. Thorne imitated his every movement, and was soon in the saddle.

"Now," said Lal Vak, "slap your gawr on the neck and pull up on the rod. He'll do the rest."

Thorne did as directed, and his mount responded with alacrity. It ran swiftly forward for about fifty feet, then with a tremendous napping of its huge, membranous wings, it took off, lurching violently at first, so that the Earthman was compelled to seize the saddle pommel in order to keep from falling off.

After he had reached a height of about two thousand feet, Lal Vak relaxed the lift on his guiding rod and settled down to a straightaway flight. Thorne kept close behind him.

When they had flown for what Thorne judged was a distance of about twenty-five miles, he noticed ahead of them a number of cylindrical buildings of various sizes, with perfectly flat roofs, built around a small lake, or lagoon. The oasis on which it was situated had a man-made look, as both it and the lagoon it encircled were perfectly square. The cylindrical buildings and the high wall surrounding the square inclosure shone in the sunlight like burnished metal.

Rising from and descending to the shores of the lagoon were a number of riders mounted on gawrs. And as they drew near, there flew up from the inclosure a mighty airship. No passengers were visible, but a number of small round windows in the sides of the body indicated their positions.

Lal Vak's mount now circled and then volplaned straight toward the margin of the lagoon. Thorne's gawr followed. As it alighted with a scarcely perceptible jar, an attendant came running up, saluted Thorne by raising his hand, palm-inward, to the level of his forehead, and took charge of his mount, making it kneel by tugging at one wing.

Thorne returned the salute and seeing that Lal Vak had dismounted, followed his example. As he stood on his feet a sudden dizziness assailed him. He braced himself to walk away with Lal Vak as if there were nothing the matter.

The scientist led him toward one of the smaller buildings, which Thorne now saw were made of blocks of a translucent material like clouded amber, cemented together with some transparent product.

As they were about to enter the circular door of the building, two men came hurrying out, and one lunged heavily against Thorne. Harry suppressed a groan with difficulty, for the fellow's elbow had come in violent contact with his wound.

14

Instantly the man who had jostled him, a huge fellow with a flat nose, beetling brows and a prognathous jaw, turned and spoke rapidly to him, his hand on his sword hilt.

Lal Vak whispered in Thorne's ear. "This is regrettable. The fellow claims you purposely jostled him, and challenges you to a duel. You must fight, or be forever branded a coward."

"Must I fight him here and now?"

"Here and now. Doctor Morgan told me you were a good swordsman. That is fortunate, for this fellow is a notorious killer."

Both men drew their swords simultaneously. Thorne endeavored to raise his blade to engage that of his adversary, but found he was without strength. His sword dropped from nerveless fingers and clattered to the pavement.

A sardonic grin came to the face of his opponent. Then he contemptuously raised his weapon and slashed the Earthman's cheek with the keen, saw-edged blade.

For an instant Thorne felt that searing pain. Then he pitched forward on his face and all went black.

CHAPTER 3

Thorne woke to a weirdly beautiful sight. Two full moons were shining down on him from a black sky in which the stars sparkled like brilliant jewels. He was lying on a bed which was suspended by four chains on a single large flexible cable which depended from the ceiling, and had his view of the sky through a large circular window.

He turned on his side, the better to look around him, and as he did so, saw Lal Vak seated on a legless chair suspended, like his bed, on a single cable which was fastened to the ceiling.

"Hello, Lal Vak," he said. "What happened?"

"I regret to inform you that you are in disgrace. If you had told me, before the duel, that you were weak from loss of blood, I could have delayed the meeting. It was only after I had brought you here that I discovered your wound, and by that time the news had gone about that you were afraid—that you had dropped your sword when faced by Sel Han."

"Sel Han! Why, that's the man Doctor Morgan wanted me to kill!"

"The same. On Earth he was Frank Boyd, a robber of mines and a jumper of claims, so the doctor informed me."

"I'll challenge Sel Han as soon as I'm up and around again. That ought to square everything, and if I win, why, the first part of my mission will have been accomplished."

"Unfortunately," replied the scientist, "that will be impossible. According to our Martian code, it would be unethical for you, under any circumstances, to provoke another duel with Sel Han. He, on the other hand, may insult or humiliate you all he likes, so long as he uses no physical violence, and does not have to stand challenge from you, for he is technically the victor."

"Then what am I to do?"

"That will rest with Sheb Takkor. As Borgen Takkor, you are, of course, son of Sheb, the Rad of Takkor. If he were to die, your name would become Sheb. As it is, you are the Zorad of Takkor. Zorad, in your language, might be translated viscount, and Rad, earl. The titles, of course, no longer have meaning, except that they denote noble blood, as the Swarm has changed all that."

"The Swarm?"

Lal Vak nodded.

"I can think of no other English equivalent for our word Kamud. The Kamud is the new order of government which took control of Xancibar about ten Martian years, or nearly nineteen Earth years ago. At that time, like other Martian vilets, or empires, of the present day, we had a Vil, or emperor. Although his office was hereditary, he could be deposed at any time by the will of the people, and a new Vil elected.

"For the most part, our people were satisfied. But there suddenly rose into power a man named Irintz Tel. He taught that an ideal community could be attained by imitating the communal life of the black bees. Under his system the individuals exist for the benefit of the community, not the community for the benefit of the individuals.

"Irintz Tel did not gather many followers, but those who flocked to his banner were vociferous and vindictive. At length, they decided to establish their form of government by force. Hearing this, Miradon, our Vil, abdicated rather than see his people involved in a civil war. He could have crushed the upstart, of course, but many lives would have been lost, and he preferred the more peaceful way.

"As soon as Miradon Vil was gone, Irintz Tel and his henchmen seized the reins of government in Dukor, the capital of Xancibar. After considerable fighting, he established the Kamud, which now owns all land, buildings, waterways, mines and commercial enterprises within our borders. He promised us annual elections, but once he was firmly established as Dixtar of Xancibar, this promise was repudiated. Theoretically, like all other citizens, Irintz Tel owns nothing except his personal belongings. But actually, he owns and controls all of Xancibar in the name of the Kamud, and has the absolute power of life and death over every citizen."

"What do people think of this arrangement?" asked Thorne. "Do they submit to such tyranny?"

"They have no choice," replied Lal Vak. "Irintz Tel rules with an iron hand. His spies are everywhere. And those detected speaking against his regime are quickly done away with.

"Some are executed, charged with some trumped-up offense, usually treason to the Kamud. Men in high places are often challenged and slain by Irintz Tel's hired swordsmen. Others are sent to the mines, which means that they will not live long. I will leave you, now. You must sleep."

"My wounds—I had forgotten them." Thorne raised his hand to his face where the sword of Sel Han had slashed him. He felt no soreness, only a porous pumicelike protrusion traveling the length of the gash. The wound in his side was covered with a similar substance.

"I had them dressed as soon as you were brought here," said the scientist. "They should not pain you, now."

"They don't. And what a strange dressing."

"It is rjembal, a flexible aromatic gum which is antiseptic, protects the wound from infection, and is porous enough to absorb seepage. Wounds closed with this gum usually heal quickly, painlessly, and without leaving scars.

"I go now. Sleep well, and to-morrow I will come to give you your first lesson in our language."

Early the next morning Thorne was awakened. He saw the white-haired Lal Vak smiling down at him. Behind him stood an orderly, who carried a large bowl which he placed on a tripod beside the bed. The orderly saluted and withdrew.

The bowl was divided into sections like a scooped-out grapefruit. In one section reposed several slices of grilled food. In another was a whole raw fruit, purple in color, and cubical in shape. In the third was a hollow cube containing an aromatic pink beverage.

Thorne sampled one of the grilled slices. The flavor baffled him, as it did not appear to be either flesh or vegetable. Having finished the strange grilled food, he tasted the pink beverage. It was slightly bitter and about as acid as a ripe orange. A sip sent an instant glow through his veins.

"What's this stuff?" he asked.

"Pulcho. A single cup is stimulating, but many are intoxicating."

Thorne finished the beverage, and Lal Vak instantly set about teaching him the things he must know in order to establish himself as Borgen Takkor.

Although Thorne's wounds healed in a few days, Lal Vak used them as a pretense to keep him in his room for about twenty. The Earthman learned the language quickly, for stored in the braincells of the Martian body which had become his were the recollections of all the sounds and their meanings.

One day an orderly came to announce that there was a man below calling himself Yirl Du, who asked to see Sheb Takkor.

"Let him come up," said Lal Vak. When the orderly had gone out he said to Thorne: "You heard what he said? He asked for Sheb Takkor."

"Yes. What does it mean?"

"It means that Sheb Takkor, father of Borgen Takkor, is dead. Hence, you are Sheb Takkor. This is one of the Takkor retainers who knows you, so call him by name when he appears before us."

A moment later, a short, stocky man entered the room. His features were coarse, but kindly. He raised one huge hand in salute, saying: "I shield my eyes, my lord Sheb, Rad of Takkor."

Thorne smiled and returned his salute. "Greetings, Yirl Du. This is my instructor, Lal Vak."

"I shield my eyes, excellency."

"You forget that under the Kamud all men are equal," said Lal Vak, returning his salute, "and one man no longer says to another: 'I shield my eyes,' 'my lord,' or 'excellency.'"

"I do not forget that I am hereditary Jen of the Takkor Free Swordsmen, nor that Sheb Takkor is my liege. From our isolated position, we of Takkor know little of the Kamud. We have submitted to it because our Rad, emulating Miradon Vil, saw fit to do so. So long as Takkor Rad rules us, though he is only the agent of the Kamud, we are content, and life goes on much as usual."

"You have come to escort your new Rad back to Takkor, I presume."

"That is my purpose, excellency."

"Then suppose you see about the gawrs while we make ready for the journey. I will accompany your Rad, and spend a few days with him."

"I go, excellency." Yirl Du saluted and withdrew.

"Strange," said Thorne, when he had gone. "He said nothing about the death of Sheb Takkor, the elder."

"His words conveyed the tidings," said Lal Vak. "A dead man's friends or relatives must not speak of him nor of his death until his ashes have been ceremonially scattered."

"When will that take place?"

"Upon your arrival. As his son and successor, you should be present at the ceremony. When it is completed, you may talk as freely as you like."

While they were talking both men had belted on their weapons and adjusted their head-cloaks. They descended to the courtyard and crossed to the lagoon, where Yirl Du waited with three gawrs attended by orderlies.

Lal Vak edged close to him. "Watch Yirl Du and me, and set your course as we do," he whispered. "You will be supposed to lead but as you don't know the way you will have to depend on one or the other of us for guidance."

In a few moments all was in readiness. The three ungainly mounts trotted forward, spread their membranous wings and took to the air.

By glancing right and left at his two companions, Thorne was easily able to gauge their course, and steer his bird-beast accordingly. They set out in a direction which he judged was due west.

Then, far ahead, Thorne saw a straight, high wall which stretched as far as he could see to the north and south. It was constructed of black stone, and at intervals of about a half mile towers built from the same material projected above it. The aqueduct which they were following led straight up to and entered this wall. As they drew near it, armed men became visible, patrolling the battlements.

Soon Thorne was able to catch a glimpse of what lay beyond the wall. First there was the glint of water in a broad canal, then the rich green of luxuriant vegetation, dotted here and there with the gleam of cylindrical crystal dwellings, and sloping in a series of terraces to a much wider canal than the first. Beyond this in the dim distance another series of terraces ascended to another elevated canal as high as the first, flanked by a wall like the one over which they were flying.

Beyond the second wall they encountered desert once more, and for several hours continued their flight toward the west. Then the contour of the ground beneath them changed abruptly. It was as if they were on the shore of a vast ocean from which the water had suddenly evaporated. First they passed over rugged cliffs, than a gently sloping beach strewn with sand and boulders. This presently dipped sharply to what was now a marshy lowland, a vast expanse of shallow water dotted and streaked with patches of green vegetation.

So absorbed was Thorne that he did not notice the menace that had crept silently up behind him. A shout from Lal Vak and a backward gesture caused him to turn in time to see a cloaked and masked warrior mounted on a swiftly flying gawr in the act of hurling a javelin at him. Behind his assailant he caught a fleeting glimpse of four more riders. He dodged just in time to avoid the barbed weapon. As it whizzed past him he whirled his gawr, then seized one of his own javelins and hurled it at his attacker.

The rider avoided Thorne's shaft with ease, and in a moment more was above him with drawn sword. Thorne whipped out his own weapon, parried a vicious head-cut, and countered with a swift slash at the neck of his assailant. The blow fell true, nearly severing the fellow's head from his body.

In the meantime, Lal Vak and Yirl Du were engaged in a lively conflict. Thorne saw the powerful Jen of the Free Swordsmen hurl a javelin with such force that it passed completely through the body of his nearest enemy. Lal Vak was fighting a sword duel with another of the attackers. The two who remained each sought a single encounter, one with Yirl Du and the other with Thorne.

The Earthman's new assailant hurled a javelin which fell short. He reached for another, and drew it back for a throw just as Thorne hurled his weapon mightily. The fellow tried to throw and dodge at the same time. He ducked low, but not low enough. Thorne's javelin struck him in the eye. His own weapon flew wide of the mark, but struck a wingjoint of the Earthman's mount.

A moment later Thorne found himself out of the saddle dangling by his safety chains, while his crippled gawr, fluttering futilely with its uninjured wing, turned over and over in the air as they hurtled swiftly toward the marsh, two thousand feet below.

CHAPTER 4

As his bird-beast turned over and over with him in the air, Thorne, swinging at the ends of his safety chains, saw that they were falling toward a small lake in the midst of the marsh with fearful velocity. As they neared the water the crippled gawr made valiant efforts to right itself, and managed to change the last few hundred feet to a glide and a dive.

They struck the water with an impact that almost robbed Thorne of consciousness. Dimly aware that he was being dragged down far below the surface of the lake, he held his breath, unhooked his safety chains, unfastened his belt and let his weapons sink. Then he fought his way swiftly to the top.

For some time the Earthman was too busy getting his breath to take note of his surroundings. Then he looked around for his mount, and saw it swimming directly away from him. Although the gawr was moving at a speed which he could not possibly hope to equal, he was about to set out in futile pursuit when a huge and terrible reptilian head suddenly reared itself between them, a scaly, silver gray head balanced on a thin, spiny neck. The monster looked first at the retreating gawr, then at the man, and began gliding swiftly toward him.

It was manifest from the start that he could not hope to outstrip his fearful aquatic enemy. As he forged ahead he glanced back from time to time, and saw that the monster was swiftly gaining on him.

With the shore but two hundred feet distant, he felt his last ounce of strength ebbing. Then just ahead of him he noticed a tiny ripple in the water, and there emerged a pair of jaws like those of a crocodile, but larger than those of any crocodile he had ever seen or heard of. There followed a broad, flat head, and thick neck, both covered with glossy fur, the head black, the neck ringed with a bright yellow band.

Hemmed thus between the two aquatic monsters, he plunged beneath the surface and dived under the oncoming beast, remaining under water until compelled to return to the surface for air.

When he had shaken the water out of his eyes, Thorne saw that the two monsters had met, and were engaged in a terrific struggle. The silver-gray scales of the one which had been following him flashed in the sun as it endeavored to shake off its smaller adversary which had seized it by the lower lip.

Suddenly it reared its head until the black-furred creature was drawn completely out of the water, and he saw that the latter was a web-footed animal about as large as a full-grown terrestrial lion, with short legs and a leathery, paddle-shaped tail which was edged with sharp spines. With the exception of the tail and claws, the body was covered with fur.

21

Thorne expected to see the smaller creature instantly slain. Instead, with a speed his eye could scarcely follow, it avoided the lunge of that terrible head, and turning, seized the slender, stalklike neck of its adversary in its own relatively large jaws. One powerful crunch, and the battle was over.

So absorbed had he been in this strange battle that Thorne had momentarily forgotten the peril that menaced him. Now, as the victor turned from the carcass of its vanquished enemy and swam straight toward him, he struck out for the shore, essaying the fast overhand stroke he had previously used on the surface, but his weary muscles had reached the limit of their endurance. Better death by drowning than in those horrible jaws. He filled his lungs and dived. At a depth of about fifteen feet he found a large water plant to which he clung with his last remaining strength.

But it seemed he was not even to be given his choice of deaths. Suddenly he became aware of a dark object in the green water above him. Then a huge pair of jaws closed around his waist, and with a deft twist, broke his hold on the water plant. A moment later he was lifted clear of the water.

The creature was carrying him swiftly toward the shore. He guessed that the monster was taking him to its lair, but on looking up, saw that it was heading directly toward the mouth of a narrow bayou. There, to his astonishment, he saw a small, flat boat, and standing in the boat a slender girl, who cried, "Good old Tezzu. Careful! Hold him gently."

Thorne's astonishment increased, for it was obvious that the girl was talking to the creature that carried him. Moreover, he assumed from her speech that she had sent this monster out to save his life.

The stern of the little craft sloped toward the water, and it was to this that the animal brought him. The girl seized a leg and an arm, and her efficient beast placed its snout beneath his body and rolled him into the boat.

Thorne essayed to sit up, but fell back weakly. Dimly, as through a haze, he saw the girl toss a rope to the beast, then felt the tug as the boat was towed ahead. The girl sat down, raised his head from the bottom of the boat and propped it in her lap.

"Who—who are you?" he asked.

She seemed surprised. "You do not know me?"

He stared hard. "I can scarcely see you. That haze . . ."

"Don't try. Close your eyes and try to sleep. Later we will talk."

It was easy for Thorne to obey her. It was good to lie there and relax with that gentle hand on his forehead.

Presently, opening his eyes, he saw that they were gliding through a narrow channel in the marsh. Trees hung over the water, their branches so interlaced and festooned with moss and lianas that only occasional shafts of sunlight penetrated to the surface.

Thorne glanced up at the girl. By any standard she was unquestionably beautiful, with her slightly tip-tilted nose, her glossy black hair, and her dark brown eyes shaded by long curling lashes. Though she was small and slender she was undoubtedly athletic. Her sole articles of apparel were a narrow band of soft leather which incased her small, firm breasts, a cincture of the same material about her smooth, tanned thighs, and the belt from which her sword, dagger and mace were suspended.

It was when he caught a glimpse of the clear sky through a rift in the branches that Thorne suddenly thought of Lal Vak and Yirl Du. He sat up abruptly.

"What's wrong?" the girl asked.

"I must go back at once."

The girl looked puzzled. "Back? How? Where? What do you mean?"

"Back to the lake where I left my friends fighting. If they survived they will be searching for me."

She shook her head. "It is too late. As it is we will barely make shelter before sundown. Tomorrow, if you like, I will take you back."

"But tomorrow will be too late. They will think me dead."

"Then, Borgen, they will be the more pleasantly surprised when you return to Castle Takkor."

"Not Borgen, Sheb."

For a moment she regarded him with a look of shocked surprise. Then sudden tears swelled in her eyes. "Has the ceremony been performed?"

"No. I was on my way to attend it with Lal Vak and Yirl Du when we were attacked, and you rescued me."

"Oh."

Thorne now realized that she must have been very well acquainted with Sheb Takkor the elder, and that she undoubtedly knew far more about the man whose place he had taken than he did himself. He wondered what her relationship had been with Borgen Takkor.

Suddenly the girl seized a long, barbed spear which lay in the bottom of the boat, and lunged at something she saw in the rushes. Then, before Thorne could rise to help her, she drew a huge iridescent beetle about three feet long into the boat. Plunging the point of the spear into the planking to keep it from escaping, she then put an end to the impaled insect's struggles by splitting its armored head with her mace. This done, she turned to the Earthman with a smile.

"We will fare well this evening. Now I can prepare your favorite dish."

Thorne looked askance at the beetle and began to have misgivings as to what his favorite dish would be like.

At this moment the beast towing the boat ran up on a small island, dragging it after him onto a sloping beach that bore the marks of many landings.

"Enough, Tezzu," called the girl. The creature dropped the tow-rope and came cavorting down to the boat like an affectionate dog, to be petted.

"You may bring the anuba, Sheb," said the girl. "Tezzu will carry the javelins."

Thorne judged that the anuba was the beetle. He withdrew the point of the spear from the planking while the girl handed the sheaf of javelins to her beast, then shouldered the heavy insect and followed her up a narrow path that wound through the undergrowth.

After walking about two hundred feet they came to a small cylindrical hut, made from stout posts driven into the ground in a compact circle and chinked with clay. The flat roof was made from the same crude materials, and the circular door was a thick cross section of an immense log.

"Don't you remember this camp, Sheb?"

"I . . ." Thorne was trying to frame a reply when, to his astonishment, the door flew open. A slender, spidery arm shot out and seized the girl by the wrist, jerking her through the opening. Then the door slammed shut.

Almost at the same instant a net dropped over the Earthman, jerking him backward. As he struggled in its enveloping meshes, he saw Tezzu drop the sheaf of javelins and with a roar of rage dash straight at the door where she had disappeared.

CHAPTER 5

Thorne was still carrying the beetle over his shoulder, hanging on the long spear. He thrust upward with the spear. The beetle prevented it from slipping through the meshes, and with the long handle he was able to raise the net and pitch it back over his head.

Scarcely had he freed himself when he saw descending from the branches of the surrounding trees six grotesque specimens of humanity. Not one of them was more than five feet tall. Their skins were bright yellow in color, and their spindly arms and legs branched out from bodies that were almost globular. Their Mongoloid features were surmounted by queer pagoda-shaped helmets of yellow metal and their bodies were protected by armor.

As they converged on him, shouting wildly, they brandished long, slightly curved swords with blunt ends, small oval guards and hilts long enough to be grasped in both hands.

Thorne ran his nearest foe through with the long spear which still held the carcass of the anuba beetle. The barbed point stuck, leaving him weaponless for the instant. Then he leaped forward, seized the sword dropped by his fallen enemy, and came on guard in time to meet the attack of the next.

Swiftly parrying a lightning cut at his legs which would instantly have laid him at the mercy of his attackers, he countered with a sudden moulinet which sheared down through the left shoulder of his second adversary, inflicting a mortal wound.

The four that remained seemed taken aback by this display of the Earthman's swordplay, and now approached him more warily. They were closing in on him from all sides when Tezzu gave up his attempts to tear down the door of the hut and suddenly rushed to Thorne's assistance.

A leap, a crunch of those powerful jaws, and one foeman fell with his head crushed. At the same time Thorne's sword disemboweled another of his antagonists. With shrieks of terror, the two survivors turned and fled. But the beast, despite its short legs, pursued them with incredible swiftness. One went down with his head between those relentless jaws and the last, catching a liana, scampered up for a little way only to be pulled down and as swiftly dispatched.

Thorne now rushed to the door of the hut and flung himself against it, but it remained immovable. Inside he heard the sound of clashing blades. A moment later he heard the inner bolt slide back and the door was flung open.

He was about to spring through the opening when he saw the girl framed in the doorway, dagger in one hand and sword in the other, both dripping blood. Behind her, barely visible in the dim light of the interior, lay one dead and one dying foeman.

"Why—why, I thought . . ." stammered Thorne, lowering his point.

The girl smiled amusedly and stepped out of the hut. "So you believed these clumsy Ma Gongi had cut me down. Really, Sheb, I gave you credit for a better memory. Have you forgotten the many times Thaine's blade has bested yours?"

So her name is Thaine, mused Thorne. Aloud he said: "Your demonstration has been most convincing. Yet I have not lost my ambition to improve my swordsmanship, and I should be grateful for further instruction."

"No better time than now. Still, I have you at a disadvantage, since you hold an inferior weapon."

"It is a handicap which a man should accord a girl," Thorne replied.

"Not one *this* girl requires."

She sheathed her dagger and extended her blade. Thorne engaged it with his captured weapon which, though more heavy and clumsy, was somewhat similar to a saber.

He instantly found that he had to deal with the swiftest and most dexterous fencer he had ever encountered, and time after time he barely saved himself from being touched.

"It seems your stay at the military school has improved your swordsmanship," said the girl, cutting, thrusting, and parrying easily—almost effortlessly. "In the old days I would have touched you long ere this. Yet, you but prolong the inevitable."

"The inevitable," replied Thorne, "is sometimes perceptible only by deity. For instance, this"—beating sharply on her blade, then catching it on his with a rotary motion—"has often been known to end a conflict."

Wrenched from her grasp by his impetuous attack, her sword went spinning into the undergrowth.

Instead of taking her defeat badly, Thaine actually beamed. "You have developed into a real swordsman, old comrade! I am so glad I could almost kiss you."

"That," Thorne answered, recovering her weapon for her, "is a reward which should fire any man to supreme endeavor."

"It is evident that you have mastered courtly speech as well as fencing. And now I will prepare your favorite dish for you." She called the brute. "Here, Tezzu," indicating the bodies. "Take these away."

Thorne marveled at its intelligence, when it instantly took up one of the corpses.

"A smart beast, that," he said.

"He is the most intelligent of all my father's dalfs. That's why I always take him with me when I hunt."

While Tezzu carried the bodies away and dropped them into the stream, Thaine took her mace and chopped off the two thick hind legs of the beetle. From these, she lopped the thighs, and splitting the shells open, extracted two cylinders of white meat. With her dagger she sliced these into small, round steaks, piling them neatly on a broad leaf, then carried it into the hut.

Thorne followed her in. "May I help?"

"I'd like some water," she replied. "Fill the big jar, please." She indicated a large square jar which stood beside the mud fireplace over which she now bent, placing faggots on a small heap of charcoal.

Thorne picked up the jar, and from its great weight was convinced that it was gold. He also noticed that the figures on the sides were of exquisite workmanship.

When he returned with water from the stream, the interior of the hut had grown quite dark, but a shaft of moonlight lit up the lithe figure of the girl, kneeling before the fireplace. He went in and placed the jar beside her.

Having arranged the faggots to her satisfaction, she took a small bottle of sparkling powder from a pouch attached to her belt, and emptied a few grains on the wood. Then, dipping a cup into the jar, she poured part of its contents on the powder. Thorne was amazed to see the powder and the surrounding wood wherever the water had touched it burst into instant flame.

With the fire blazing merrily, the girl now dipped several cupfuls of water from the jar into a smaller container, dropped into it a handful of red berries taken from another jar, and set the mixture against the blaze. Then she arranged the steaks she had cut on a grill made from crossed metal rods.

Tezzu came in, his immense mouth full of faggots, which he dropped beside her. Then he touched her elbow with his nose. She turned and patted his head. "Good boy. Bring more."

Obediently the beast turned and trotted out into the moonlight.

By the time the steaks were broiled, Tezzu had brought in a considerable quantity of wood. After removing her broiler, Thaine threw more fuel on the coals. From the vessel into which she had put the red berries she now filled two cubical golden cups with a steaming pink liquid. Then, using a wide leaf for a platter, she piled it high with the grilled steaks, set two other bits of leaf on the floor for plates.

"Come, Sheb. The banquet is ready for the victors."

Thorne sat opposite her and took the steaming cup from her hand. He had guessed that the beverage it contained was pulcho, and a sip confirmed this. Then

27

came the realization that the time had arrived for him to simulate a liking for his "favorite dish."

"It is a banquet fit for a mighty conqueror," he said, reaching for one of the grilled steaks. He bit out a portion and instantly recognized the flavor. It was the same as that of the broiled food which had been served him for his first breakfast on Mars.

He had noted a swift, curious glance on the part of Thaine, when she had seen him take up his steak in his hand. Now he saw that she used her dagger as a fork to convey a slice to her leaf-plate, and that she cut off a small piece which she raised to her mouth with her fingers.

Obviously he had made a Martian social error.

Suddenly the girl leaned forward. "Just who are you, masquerading as Sheb Takkor?"

For a moment Thorne was speechless with surprise. Then he replied, "Ever since I met you I have been wanting to tell you, but the consideration of a duty restrained me."

"A duty?"

"Yes. To friends who helped me."

"And now, am I not—another friend who has helped you?"

"Decidedly! Yet, I wonder if you will believe me. I can scarcely believe myself, that I am here."

"Don't be too sure that I would not believe. I *know*. You are—Hahr Ree Thorne, and you were born on the planet, Dhu Gong, which you call Earth."

"How did you know that?"

"Borgan told me what he was going to do," she replied. "I did not believe it possible, but now I know. You are so different. And you do not understand some of our Martian customs."

"For instance, my manner of eating? Pray tell me where I erred."

"Having a dagger, you would have waited for me to take the first morsel," she said. "Lacking it, you would wait for me to hand you mine, then use it as I used it."

"I have been a boor."

"Not at all. One cannot be expected to know the customs of a new world without some instruction."

When both had eaten all they wanted, the remainder was tossed to the waiting dalf. Then the girl rose, closed and bolted the door, and selecting two large furs from a pile against the wall, gave one to the Earthman and spread the other on the floor before the fire.

"It is time for sleep," she said. Then, without another word, she lay down on the fur and drawing its folds about her, closed her eyes.

As he spread his fur and rolled himself therein, he again mentally compared his former fianceé to the girl who slept calmly there beside him, and the comparison was overwhelmingly favorable to Thaine.

CHAPTER 6

Thorne was awakened by a touch on his brow. He looked up into the eyes of Thaine.

"We must begin our journey if you would make Castle Takkor by midday," she said.

He threw off his fur and stood up. "I'm ready," he announced.

"First we will eat," she told him.

When they had finished, the girl began packing the utensils and furs together. Thorne helped her to make two large bundles of them, which Tezzu carried down to the boat.

"The Ma Gongi have discovered this camp," she told him, "so it must be abandoned forever."

"But where will you go?"

"I have many better places hidden in the marsh," she replied. "This was merely an outpost."

They gathered up the weapons and went outside. Then the girl poured a small quantity of the sparkling firepowder against the door jamb and dashed a cup of water over it. The logs instantly burst into flame, and when they reached the boat, Thorne, looking back, saw that a thick column of smoke was mounting skyward.

The morning sun was, by this time, halfway to the zenith. Most of the ice had melted in the stream. He noted, also, that many of the leaves where the sun had not yet penetrated were coated with hoar-frost that was rapidly melting into glistening beads of dew.

When they had their cargo stowed, and had taken their places, the girl tossed the tow-rope to Tezzu and indicated with a wave of her hand the direction she wished to go. He plunged into the stream and set off rapidly.

They had only gone a short distance when Thaine cried: "Look there! The boat of the Ma Gongi!"

Thorne looked in the direction she was pointing, and saw a flat boat drawn up on the bank.

"Stop, Tezzu," ordered the girl. Then: "Bring us that boat."

The beast dropped the tow-rope, and swimming in to shore, dragged the boat into the water. Then, seizing its rope he towed it out to where they drifted. Save for a bundle, wrapped in a silky covering, and a half dozen spade-shaped paddles, the boat was empty. Thorne was about to reach for the bundle when the girl checked him. "That is their food," she said, "but it will do us no good." Then she called to the dalf. "Sink it, Tezzu."

Instantly, the beast seized the side of the boat in his huge and powerful jaws. A single crunch crushed the heavy planking as if it had been an eggshell. Tezzu backed away, spitting out the slivers, and the boat filled and sank. Then he took up the tow-rope once more and proceeded on his way.

"I'm curious to know more about these Ma Gongi," Thorne said, "and this strange, forbidden food they eat."

"Legend has it that they did not originate on this planet, but, as their name indicates, on Ma Gong, the planet which now circles your world, but which revolved in an orbit of its own, between your world and mine.

"We know that there was once a mighty civilization here on Mars, and that it was destroyed in terrible catastrophe. It is just within my lifetime that our scientists have begun to uncover old records—fragments of records—and piece them together. We know now that the catastrophe came about through an interplanetary war, fought with weapons almost beyond imagination. The Ma Gongi had a cold, energy-decreasing interrotating green ray. Any substance touched by this ray would contract to less than one-hundredth of its normal size, with a corresponding increase in density.

"The toughest metals, under this ray, would become as brittle as glass and more dense than lead. But there is a limit to the contractile endurance of all matter, and once that limit is reached the atoms, which have been pushed in upon themselves, explode and disintegrate."

"And did your scientists have this weapon, too?"

"We do not know. Ma Gong was shifted from its orbit to where it now lies, and it is believed that our two moons came from some aspect of the struggle, too. We know that Ma Gong itself was rendered uninhabitable and that our own world was greatly damaged. Some of the Ma Gong must have been stranded on Mars when the war ended in mutual ruin."

"Remarkable," said Thorne.

"The Ma Gong are our enemies still," she went on. "I have often seen them. But other than them, my father, the Takkors and Yirl Du, I have seen no one except the Little People."

"The Little People?"

"They are the friends and allies of my father and me. But the Ma Gongi eat them. That is why I told you the food you saw in their boat would be useless to us. It was the flesh of one of the Little People."

"But who is your father, and why do you two live here in the marsh, instead of among your own kind?"

"My father's name is Miradon. Once he was Vil of Xancibar. There was a revolt, led by a man named Irintz Tel. In order to avoid the calamity of a civil war, my father abdicated, and fled here with me, aided by Sheb Takkor and the Jen of his Free Swordsmen, Yirl Du. These two, alone, knew where we had gone. Here my father reared me. We have been constantly harassed by the minions of Irintz Tel, and lately by the Ma Gongi as well. For three days, now, my father has been absent, and I fear that he has either been slain or captured."

"Then let me help you search for him."

"No, you must return to the castle for the ceremony, or if it has been performed, to assume your rightful place. After that, come if you will, and bring Yirl Du, but no other. He will know how to find me."

For some time now they had been gliding tortuously through a chain of shallow pools connected by narrow, half-hidden channels. Now there suddenly came into view a broad lake which mirrored at its far side an immense castle of odd and beautiful design, the translucent masonry of which gleamed like burnished gold in the sunshine. A short distance from it, and also bordering the lake, rose the cylindrical, flat-roofed buildings of a teeming city. A large number of gawrs were swimming on the lake and many boats were moored at the docks.

"This is as far as I dare take you," said Thaine. "Yonder, beside Takkor City, lies Castle Takkor. You can reach it by following the lake shore to the right."

31

Thorne rose and stretched his limbs, cramped from long sitting. Then he bent, took her hand and pressed it to his lips. She seemed startled. "Why did you do that?"

"On my world it is homage one pays to a lady at greeting or parting."

"What a queer custom," she exclaimed. "But I rather like it."

Thorne smiled. "Farewell, little comrade," he said. "Again I thank you for my life, for my entertainment, and most of all for the pleasure of having been with you. As soon as I have attended to my duties at Castle Takkor I will return with Yirl Du, and together we will search for your father."

"Deza go with you, and keep you safe from harm. I will be waiting for you and be expecting you."

Resolutely he turned away and stepped over the side of the boat. He stood there in the shallows watching until the little craft vanished around a bend in the narrow channel.

Keeping to the margin of the lake, he eventually reached the docks without mishap. Most of its occupants were fishermen, and those whose duty it was to tend the gawrs. But he saw a number of warriors standing about, and was surprised to note that they wore the insigne of the Kamud. As he made his way toward the gate which led to the castle, two of them stopped him.

"Where are you going, fellow?" asked one. "And whom do you seek?"

"I go to Castle Takkor," replied Thorne, "and whom I seek is my own affair."

"None of your insolence," growled the other soldier. "When you speak to us, you address the Kamud."

"When you speak to me, you address the Rad of Takkor," Thorne retorted. "Out of my way!"

"Sharp words call for sharper weapons," said one soldier. "Throw down your sword, or you die."

For answer, Thorne came on guard. Then both men attacked him simultaneously. While he could easily have bested either of them alone, he was sorely put to it to keep the two blades from reaching him. Presently, however, one soldier left his head unguarded. Instantly Thorne's sword sheared down through his brain.

For a moment Thorne's blade was held by that cloven skull; then, with a desperate jerk, he freed his weapon and easily disarmed his remaining foe, who instantly turned and fled, bawling lustily for help.

At this juncture a big man, resplendent in purple head-cloak and gold trappings came down the steps that led from the castle gate, followed by a group of lesser officers and a file of soldiers.

"What's all this?" he roared. "Must I have brawling on the first day of my arrival?"

Thorne looked up and recognized Sel Han, against whom the Martian code of honor now forbade him to raise his weapon. Instantly he was surrounded by warriors.

"This impostor who murdered Tir Hanus claims to be the Rad of Takkor," cried the disarmed soldier, "yet we scattered his ashes this morning."

Sel Han looked at Thorne. "You have heard the words of this soldier," he said. "Do you still cling to your preposterous claim?"

"You scattered the ashes of Sheb Takkor the elder. Not mine."

"We also scattered the ashes of Sheb Takkor the younger," replied Sel Han. "His two comrades, Lal Vak and Yirl Du, reported his death yesterday. He fell from his gawr, a distance that would crush him to pulp, therefore it is impossible that he could be alive to-day. Word was sent to Irintz Tel, and the Dixtar appointed me to administer the estates in the name of the Kamud. As we could not obtain the body of the unfortunate Rad, who fell in the marsh, we performed the ceremony by proxy, using ashes of the aromatic sebolis tree, as is the custom."

"Am I to understand from this that I am officially dead?"

"You are to understand from this that the Rad of Takkor is dead. Also, the title has been abolished. Hereafter the estates will be strictly administered in accordance with the rules of the Kamud. As to who *you* are, that has not been established. You came to us armed with a sword of the Ma Gongi, and impersonating the dead Rad. When questioned, you slew a soldier of the Kamud. Under the circumstances, it is my duty to arrest you and send you to Dukor for trial."

"You make yourself absurd by claiming that I am dead."

"Yield your sword, or you soon will be," promised Sel Han. "Seize him, men. If he resists, cut him down."

Seeing that resistance against such odds would be foolhardy, Thorne handed his sword to the nearest soldier. Another removed the medal that hung around his neck. Then he was led away by two warriors. They took him into the castle courtyard, where one of the large flying machines he had previously seen stood ready to take off. He was hustled up a set of metal steps and into the body of the craft, where a score of prisoners, guarded by two armed warriors, were chained by metal collars to rings in the wall. A collar was snapped around his neck.

CHAPTER 7

Thorne's journey was not a pleasant one.

Like the other prisoners, the Earthman was compelled by the lurching of the ship to keep a tight hold on his chain with both hands, and thus ease the sudden jerks on his metal collar that would otherwise have choked him. Consequently he was thankful when, after more than an hour of riding, he sensed that the ship was settling, then felt the shock of its landing.

A moment later the door was flung open by one of the guards and the folding metal steps were dropped. The other guard opened the prisoners' collars, one by one, with a key he carried, and ordered them out the door. Thorne, the third to step out, saw that they were in a large walled inclosure in which were several hundred men, some lying on the ground or lolling against the walls, others pacing up and down, or conversing in small groups.

At the bottom of the ladder an officer waited, attended by two soldiers, one of whom carried a bundle of metal rings. The officer was scanning a paper which the first guard had handed him, evidently a list of prisoners. As each man descended, he asked his name and checked the list. Then the soldier with the rings fastened one about the prisoner's neck and called the number engraved on the ring.

When it came Thorne's turn, the officer asked "Your name?"

"Sheb Takkor."

"What is your *real* name?"

"I have told you," Thorne replied.

The officer shrugged. "It will be so entered, though the report says you are an impostor. But that will be a matter for the judges."

He signed to the soldier with the rings, who clamped one about Thorne's neck and called the number. The soldier gave him a push that sent him stumbling into the yard, and the officer began questioning the next prisoner.

Recovering his balance, the Earthman walked morosely to the center of the inclosure. A glance about him at the high walls patrolled by heavily armed warriors convinced him that escape would be next to impossible. Beyond the walls on all sides he saw the upper stories of many cylindrical, flat-topped buildings. He concluded, from this, that he must be in the midst of a large and populous city.

Having completed his inspection of his surroundings, he found a place where he could sit and lean against the wall, and think. His case, it seemed, was well nigh hopeless.

As he sat there, Thorne noticed coming toward him a man with a huge chest and shoulders, long, ape-like arms, and abnormally short legs. With a start of surprise, he recognized the Jen of the Takkor Free Swordsmen.

"Yirl Du!" he exclaimed.

"I shield my eyes, my lord Sheb," said the Jen, "and thank Deza that you still live. Lal Vak and I thought you dead, and so reported at the castle."

"What brought you here?"

"My arrest came so suddenly," replied Yirl Du, "that I am still bewildered. I was sent here this morning charged with inciting the Free Swordsmen to revolt against the Kamud."

"And should they be able to prove such an absurd charge, what will be the penalty?"

"Death. In what form, I know not. The seven dread judges of the Kamud deal out death in many fiendish forms. *Their* most merciful sentence is the stroke of the sword. Then there are the mines. A sentence to the mines is really a death sentence, for few men survive their rigors for many days."

"And what sentence do you think they will pass on me?"

"Of what is my lord accused?"

"I slew a soldier of the Kamud who attacked me. Also I am to be charged with impersonating myself, because I am officially dead. Furthermore, there is some suspicion attached to me, which I cannot fathom, because I was wearing a sword of the Ma Gongi."

Yirl Du groaned. "You might have obtained an acquittal on the first two counts, but I fear this latter spells your doom. Deza grant that I, Yirl Du, Jen of the Takkor Free Swordsmen, may never live to see my Rad die in such dishonor."

"But why should a sword of the Ma Gongi constitute such damning evidence?"

"It is believed," the Jen told him, "that the Ma Gongi are plotting to overthrow the Old Race—to conquer all Mars. There have been persistent rumors that one of the archaeologists has unearthed the secret of the deadly green ray.

"Although we would not dare to publicly voice our suspicions, there are also those among us who suspect Sel Han of plotting with the Ma Gongi. He has so wormed himself into the good graces of Irintz Tel that a word breathed against him would bring instant disaster to almost any man.

"It is said, also, that the Dixtar intends to wed his daughter Neva to this arch-plotter, and that through marriage with her he will eventually succeed to the dixtarship of Xancibar."

"It is obvious that this Sel Han is indeed a menace to all mankind," said Thorne.

"I have a further suspicion," went on Yirl Du, "born when you told me of the disappearance of Thaine's father. Miradon Vil, a prisoner, would be of inestimable value to Sel Han in his plans for conquest. With the Vil in his power, he could hold the royalists as well as the Kamud in the hollow of his hand. A colony of the Ma Gongi inhabits a part of the marsh not far from Miradon's hiding place. And it may well be that they, at the instigation of their ally, Sel Han, have captured the Vil and are holding him in some secret hiding place."

Thorne was about to reply when a shrill whistle sounded.

"Come," said Yirl Du. "That was the food signal, and the last ten men in line always go hungry."

They both sprang forward to where a long line of prisoners was forming before a table containing some small cakes and cubical cups of pulcho, presided over by four orderlies who had already begun to hand a cup and cake to each man, under the watchful eyes of the half dozen soldiers with drawn swords. Thorne saw, on looking back, that there were exactly ten men behind him.

Shuffling forward with the others, he was surprised to feel a powerful hand clapped on his shoulder. Before he could offer the slightest resistance, he was spun around, and found himself walking behind the man who had previously been just behind him.

Thorne seized the brawny arm of the man who had supplanted him and swung him around. He had a swift glimpse of a glaring face, crisscrossed by a frightful pattern of livid scars. Then he drove a smashing right hook to the point of the jaw that sent the man reeling backward to the ground.

In a moment the fellow began to recover from the effect of the blow, and sat up looking about him. Suddenly spying Thorne, he shook his bullet head, then lurched to his feet, and charged.

Thorne turned at the sound, and prepared to meet the shock of the attack. With both arms outstretched, the man attempted to seize him, but a blow in the solar plexus followed by a swift uppercut downed him again.

Instantly, Yirl Du, who had drained his pulcho cup and was munching his cake, tossed the food aside and sprang forward. "Let me handle this beast, my lord. He is Sur Det, the most dreaded duelist and assassin in all Xancibar."

By this time most of the prisoners were crowding around, talking excitedly while they munched and drank.

"Swords!" some one shouted. "Bring swords!"

A group of guards came shouldering through the crowd, making way for a handsome fellow who wore the purple cloak of an officer of the Kamud.

"What's this, Sur Det?" he asked. "Fighting again?"

Sur Det scrambled to his feet and saluted. "That fellow," he said, glaring at Thorne, "has twice assaulted me. I ask settlement by swords, which is my right according to the prison rules."

The officer turned to Thorne. "What say you? Do you, also, desire settlement by swords?"

"I do," the Earthman replied.

"Obviously you have not heard of the prowess of Sur Det," said the officer. "But on your own head be your decision. Give them swords, soldiers, and let a circle be formed."

CHAPTER 8

As he stood, sword in hand, before his scar-faced opponent, Thorne was hooted by the multitude. A few who had heard of his supposed cowardice in his duel with Sel Han, quickly spread the word.

"Don't puncture him too quickly, Sur Det," called one.

"Slice him neatly," shouted another. "Let us see how good a meat-cutter you are."

They saluted. Then Sur Det, instead of engaging Thorne's extended blade as was the custom, avoided it and attacked with a swift lunge. The Earthman was barely able to save his life by side-stepping the point.

But Sur Det had left himself completely uncovered. Thorne now had but to extend his point, and the duel would be over. He started the lunge, but instead of sending the blade home, with a deft motion of his wrist cut the Martian symbol for the digraph "sh," a perpendicular line with a short hook to the right at the bottom.

A murmur of surprise went up from the crowd at this, for they knew he had his enemy at his mercy. Both men recovered. After a bewildering swirl of blades Thorne found a second opening, and instead of piercing the heart of his antagonist, slashed two horizontal lines beside the first character, the Martian symbol for "e."

"He's writing his name on the killer!" cried a spectator.

"Write him a love letter!" yelled another.

"Draw us a picture!" howled a third.

When Thorne marked his chest for the second time without inflicting death, Sur Det began to realize that this strange young swordsman from Takkor, whom he had expected to slay so easily, was only playing with him. With that realization, he went berserk with fear.

Thorne met the attack that followed, merely parrying and sidestepping until he felt his opponent's wrist begin to weaken. Then with a graceful, easy lunge, he carved the last symbol of his Martian name on that barrel chest, the "b."

At this, the crowd roared its applause, but Thorne had not yet finished; he suddenly beat down his opponent's blade with a sharp blow close to the guard—then caught it, bound it with his own blade, and with a sudden twirling wrench, sent it flashing away over the heads of the spectators.

For a moment the bewildered killer stood looking in blank amazement. Then, with a shriek of terror, he turned and fled. Thorne followed closely at his heels, spanking him soundly—with the flat of his sword until the creature fell down and begged for mercy.

"Puncture the boastful bladder and let out the wind," a spectator shouted.

"Carve your name on his craven heart," cried another.

Satisfied that the killer had been sufficiently humbled, Thorne returned to where the young officer stood, and saluted.

"I am obliged to you for this diversion," he said, tendering the sword.

"The obligation is entirely ours," replied the officer, taking the weapon. "I have never seen such marvelous sword-work, nor, I am convinced, has any one in all Xancibar. And now, to the victor goes the reward. Ho, orderly!"

At this a man came up, bearing a steaming jar of pulcho, a cup and a great platter heaped with cakes.

"What's this?" asked Thorne.

"The prize," smiled the officer, taking the jar from the orderly and filling a cup which he handed to the Earthman. "I regret that so distinguished a swordsman and so gallant a gentleman may not be more suitably rewarded. But this, after all, is a prison."

"To your long life," said Thorne, draining his cup. Then he turned to the orderly. "Distribute the cakes and the rest of the pulcho to the ten who were not served, including my defeated opponent."

At this added evidence of the generosity of their new champion, the multitude shouted its approbation. More than a half hour elapsed before Thorne was able to get away from his numerous admirers and sit alone once more with Yirl Du.

"That was a marvelous fight, my lord," said the Jen. "It will surely remove the stigma attached to your name by that unfortunate incident at the military school. The great pity of it is that it comes at a time when death by order of the Kamud is almost certain to be your lot."

"It will be certain enough if Sel Han has his way."

"We have many good reasons to kill that flat-nosed traitor," replied Yirl Du, "and there are two which I have not related to you. One is, that among the men who attacked us in the air I recognized one of his henchmen. So it was he who sent those assassins to slay us."

"What is the other?" asked Thorne.

"I have hesitated to tell you that one, as I would not give you needless pain on what may well be your last day of life. Know, then, that Sheb Takkor the elder was murdered. I was making my last round of the castle before retiring, to see if all was well, when I noticed him seated before the fireplace in his great swinging chair, hunched over in a most unnatural position. I called to him, but he made no response. I ran to his side, and saw that he was dead. A dagger had been driven into his back up to the hilt."

"And you think it was Sel Han who struck the blow?"

"More likely one of his hired assassins. He, and no one else, had much to gain by the death of our beloved Rad. And he alone profited by it."

"Perhaps there was an enemy with a grudge."

"That is not likely. The Rad never left Takkor except to hunt in the marshes or the desert, or to secretly do what he could for our deposed sovereign and his daughter. So he had no opportunity to make enemies in other than his own raddek. And I'll swear that there was not a man, woman or child among his people who did not love and revere him. Moreover, the dagger was of foreign make and delicate workmanship, not the plain sturdy kind our Takkor folk are wont to carry. I hid it in the castle, hoping that it might some day afford us proof of the identity of the assassin."

At this juncture two guards with drawn swords in their hands stopped before Thorne.

"Are you he who calls himself Sheb Takkor?" asked one.

"I am," Thorne replied.

"The Dixtar has sent for you. Come with us."

Thorne stood up, but as he did so Yirl Du flung himself between the Earthman and the guards. "Wait! Don't take him! Take me! I am Sheb Takkor!"

One of the guards laughed contemptuously. "Out of the way, O great oaf, ere I cut you down. My comrade and I sat on the wall and saw this man defeat Sur Det, the killer. Do you think you could pass for him? Moreover, have we not eyes to read the numbers on your collars?"

Yirl Du turned to Thorne. "I fear it is the end, my lord," he groaned. He saluted. "Farewell, my lord. Deza grant you life, yet if that be not His will, a brave death."

Thorne returned the salute. "Farewell, my friend," he answered.

The Earthman was led through a gate into what was obviously one of the streets of a large city. It was paved with a tough, resilient material of a reddish-brown color, and was thronged with people and strange vehicles of many descriptions. There was one thing, however, which the vehicles all had in common. They did not travel on wheels, but ran about on multiple sets of jointed metal legs shod with balls of the resilient reddish-brown substance. The smallest of these odd vehicles had only two pairs of legs, but some of the larger ones had so many that they reminded him of gigantic caterpillars, moving smoothly and swiftly along the thoroughfare.

In a moment an open vehicle with twelve pairs of legs drew up before the gate and stopped. There were three saddle-shaped seats with high backs, one in front and two side by side in the rear. A canopy overhead shaded the passengers. The front seat was occupied by a driver in military uniform. In one of the rear seats sat the Jen of the Prison Guards.

"The Dixtar has commanded that I bring you before him," he said. "Give me your word that you will not attempt to escape while in the custody of Kov Lutas, and I will spare you the ignominy of chains."

The Earthman thought for a moment. If he gave his word, once out of the custody of Kov Lutas, he could, with honor, make the attempt.

"I give my word that I will not try to escape while in your custody."

The Jen ordered the guards to remove Thorne's prison collar, and when this was done, dismissed them with a wave of his hand. "Get in," he invited.

Thorne climbed into the vacant saddle. The driver, who sat holding two levers that projected up through the floor at either side of his saddle, now slowly moved these forward. At this, the vehicle started silently and was soon moving through the traffic at a considerable speed.

Thorne saw that when the driver wished to turn to the right he advanced the left lever and drew back the right, and that he reversed the process to turn to the left. To increase the speed, he pushed both levers forward, and to decrease it drew them backward. When they were drawn back to a certain point, the vehicle came to a full stop.

Having satisfied his curiosity regarding the vehicle, Thorne turned his attention to the strange sights about him.

Noting the Earthman's interest in his surroundings, Kov Lutas said: "Apparently this is your first visit to Dukor. Perhaps you would like to have me explain some of the sights of the city."

"I should be grateful," Thorne replied.

"Dukor is divided into four equal quarters by the intersecting triple canals, Zeelan and Corvid. We are now in the northwest quarter of the city, and about to cross the Zeelan Canal into the northeast quarter, where the palace which formerly belonged to the Vil, but is now occupied by the Dixtar, is located."

"It must be a tremendous city."

"There are approximately five million people residing in each quarter," replied Kov Lutas, "or twenty million in all. Also, we have each day about ten million transients who come on commercial or state business, or simply to visit and to see the sights. Dukor is a fair-sized city as cities go. Of course it does not seem large in comparison with Raliad, capital city of Kalsivar, which commands the intersections of four great triple canals, for Raliad is said to have a population of a hundred million."

While he was speaking they came to the approach of a tremendous arched bridge, so long they could not see the farther end of it. In a moment they were out upon it, and Thorne was looking down upon the surface of the first of the three canals which collectively bore the name of Zeelan because they occupied the same huge trench. This canal swarmed with craft of many sizes and shapes, a large number of which were discharging freight into the dock warehouses which lined its banks.

The huge central canal at the bottom of the great trench, which caught the drainage from the two upper irrigating canals, was lined with bathers of all ages who wore no clothing whatever.

The canal passed, they entered a section of the city quite similar to the one they had just left. After a drive of about half an hour in this section, they drew up before an immense and magnificent edifice.

"The Palace," said Kov Lutas. "From this point we walk."

After getting down from the vehicle, they mounted a broad flight of steps which led to the vast and ornate portico. Here they were halted and questioned by guards, who readily admitted them when shown the order of the Dixtar which Kov Lutas carried. Then, after crossing an immense busy foyer and traversing a long hallway, they came before a large circular doorway, closed by two purple curtains in which was embroidered with gold thread, the coat of arms of the Dixtar of Xancibar. Here an officer examined the order carried by Kov Lutas.

"The Dixtar is expecting you," he said. Then he beckoned to one of the guards. "Announce Kov Lutas, Jen of the Guards of Prison Number 67," he said, "and a prisoner."

CHAPTER 9

When the curtain was drawn aside, Thorne followed Kov Lutas through the doorway, and found himself in the presence of Irintz Tel.

The Dixtar, his hands clasped behind him, was pacing to and fro on a plush-padded dais that fronted a luxuriously cushioned throne, which hung on four heavy golden chains depending from the ceiling. He was a small man, sparely built and quite bald. Thin-lipped, sharp-nosed and beady-eyed, his face bore the unmistakable stamp of the zealot and reformer.

Irintz Tel paced up and down for some time without taking the slightest notice of Kov Lutas and his prisoner.

After a lapse of some minutes, Irintz Tel paused midway in his pacing and, swinging on his heel, faced Kov Lutas.

"Well?" he demanded, in a high-pitched, squeaky voice.

Kov Lutas raised both hands in salute, holding them before his face. "I shield my eyes in the glory of your presence, O mighty Dixtar of Xancibar and Commander of the Kamud."

Thorne was astounded, for he had been told that under the Kamud all salutations of this sort had been abolished.

The Earthman suddenly noticed that Irintz Tel was looking sharply at him, evidently expecting him to follow the example of the Jen; but he kept his hands down.

"Who is this ill-mannered lout you have brought into our presence, Kov Lutas?" demanded the Dixtar.

"He is Sheb Takkor, whom I bring in accordance with the Dixtar's command," replied Kov Lutas.

"His manners are execrable," said Irintz Tel, "but they can be mended, and we hear that he is a good swordsman. It may be that we will find employment for him. We are both blessed and cursed with a beautiful daughter, as you are no doubt aware."

"I have heard of the great beauty of your excellency's daughter," replied Kov Lutas, cautiously.

"It is a fatal beauty that corrupts our most loyal followers and makes traitors of our staunchest patriots. And today we are constrained to part with two more of our best swordsmen. They were her guardsmen, but they chose to let their hearts rule their heads. For such a malady, where our daughter is concerned, we have a most effective form of surgery."

"What is that, excellency?"

"In order that the heart may no longer rule the head, we separate them. A bit drastic, we will admit, but it never fails to cure. We sent for you and this prisoner because we must replace the two excellent swordsmen. Our daughter, as you know, must be well guarded.

"We will first take the case of the prisoner, here. Word came to us today of his defeat of Sur Det, the killer, so we decided to personally examine into the charges against him. He is accused, we find, of impersonating the dead Rad of Takkor, of wearing a sword of the Ma Gongi, and of slaying a soldier of the Kamud, and as evidence there have come to us this Takkor family medal," lifting it from a small taboret beside the throne, "and this sword which he was alleged to have been wearing when captured. What say you to these charges, prisoner?"

"I could not impersonate the Rad of Takkor without impersonating myself," replied Thorne. "I was reported dead because my crippled gawr fell with me after I was attacked. But we fell into a small lake. After freeing myself from the safety

43

chains and the weight of my weapons, I swam ashore. There I was attacked by a party of Ma Gongi, and after wresting the sword from one of them, beat off the others."

"We can well believe that. But why did you slay one of our soldiers?"

"Because he attacked me on my own doorstep. In answer to that charge I plead self-defense."

The Dixtar paced the dais for some time, chin on chest. Then he suddenly turned and looked at Thorne.

"We hereby declare you innocent and discharged of all liability on all three counts," he said brusquely.

"And as a recompense for the indignities which you have suffered, we raise you to the rank of Jen and appoint you night guard to our daughter Neva."

He turned to the Jen of the Prison Guards. "You also, my worthy Kov Lutas, we have decided to honor. You, henceforth, will guard our daughter by day."

The face of Kov Lutas went as suddenly pale as if a sentence of death had been passed on him.

Despite Kov Lutas's dismay, he managed to retain control of his features. "I am deeply grateful that our Dixtar has chosen to distinguish me by this honor."

Irintz Tel beckoned Thorne to him and handed him the medal. "Take back this badge of your ancient race and wear it with honor. We regret that we cannot return your title as well, but under the present social order there are no more rads. Nor can we make you our deputy, for upon hearing of your supposed death we immediately dispatched Sel Han to Takkor to represent us, as he knows our wishes and is high in our councils."

"The Dixtar is most generous," murmured Thorne.

Irintz Tel now called to the officer at the door. "Ho, Dir Hazef, conduct these two to the officers' quarters and see that they are suitably arrayed as palace Jens. On the way you will permit them to witness the fate which overtakes those who are unfaithful to their trust, and show them the Halls of Heads. Let a sword and dagger decked with the Takkor serpent be brought from the armory for the one who is weaponless, as he is entitled to carry them."

The two men saluted, and Dir Hazef conducted them to a small balcony which overlooked one of the inner courts. In the center of the court stood an officer. Dir Hazef signaled to him, and he, in turn, signaled to some one in a nearby doorway. A moment later there emerged two soldiers, driving before them two young officers with their hands bound behind them. Following the soldiers came a tall fellow bearing a long, straight-bladed sword and accompanied by a boy who carried a basket.

The two prisoners were forced to kneel in the center of the courtyard. Then the tall man stepped behind them. Once, twice, his long blade flashed in the sunlight, and with each blow a head rolled to the pavement, to be garnered by the boy with the basket.

"Those two," said Dir Hazef, "were the guards of Neva, daughter of the Dixtar. They had the good taste but the bad judgment to fall in love with her and contend for her favors." He turned, and walking to a door behind them, opened it. "Enter."

Thorne stepped through the doorway, followed by Kov Lutas and their conductor.

"This," said Dir Hazef, "is the Hall of Heads, a monument to the Dixtar's justice and a warning to those who would betray him."

They were in a long, narrow room, lined with shelves on both sides clear to the high ceiling. On the shelves stood row after row of crystal jars. Each jar was filled with clear liquid, and in the liquid floated a severed human head. There were thousands of heads of young men and old; even heads of women and children.

Thorne tore his eyes away from the exhibit with a shudder, and turning, saw that Kov Lutas had already preceded him through the doorway.

After locking the door and leading them down another corridor, Dir Hazef conducted them through a room where a number of officers sat in swinging chairs, sipping pulcho and conversing, or playing gapun, a game which consisted of rolling little engraved pellets of gold or silver at numbered holes in a board, the highest number winning all the pellets risked. Although he had never before seen Martian money, Thorne recognized at once that these pellets must be the medium of exchange.

A number of apartments opened into this officers' club room, and into one of these Dir Hazef led them. "I'll leave you here to bathe and change. Vorz, your orderly, will bring your new uniforms and weapons. You, Kov Lutas, are to go on duty at once, and Sheb Takkor will relieve you at the time of the evening meal."

The apartment was plainly but comfortably furnished with a swinging bed and a swinging chair for each man, a wardrobe and an arms rack. In one corner was a metal box about eight feet in height, one side of which stood open. It was lined throughout with a gray metal resembling block tin, and this lining was perforated with many holes. Beside it was a rack on which hung a number of wisps of what looked like dry moss.

As soon as Dir Hazef was gone, Kov Lutas began removing his clothing and weapons. "I'll bathe now, if you don't mind," he said, "as I must go on duty first."

"Of course," replied Thorne. He was puzzled as he saw no sign of a tub or bathroom.

His curiosity was soon satisfied. Kov Lutas stepped into the square metal box in the corner and drew the side shut. Immediately there was the sound of rushing water, accompanied by much gurgling, blowing and gasping. A few moments later the side swung open, and the officer emerged, dripping and rubbing the water from his eyes. Then he reached for a bunch of the moss-like material and began briskly rubbing himself.

Thorne, who had meanwhile removed his clothing, now entered the box and drew the side shut. As he moved about, he accidentally trod on a round plate in the center of the metal floor. Instantly he was surrounded by a swirl of warm, scented water which came up to his chin. The water soon receded as suddenly as it had risen, and several jets opened overhead, deluging him with a fragrant creamy lather.

After about a minute of this there was a click as of some automatic mechanism, the jets ceased to spray, and the swirling water rose once more. While it rinsed off the lather this gradually grew cooler until it reached an almost icy temperature. Another click, and it drained away automatically. He opened the side, sputtering and gasping, and blindly reached for a bundle of drying material. As soon as he had the water out of his eyes he saw that an orderly had arrived with the new uniforms, and was helping Kov Lutas into his.

Thorne rubbed himself until his skin glowed warmly. Vorz, the orderly, then assisted him to don his new uniform and buckle on his weapons. His new sword and dagger hilts were fashioned like those he had found himself wearing on his first advent on Mars, but were of gold powdered with jewels instead of plain brass. And the eyes of the serpents were large rubies.

The orderly, after bustling in with a three-legged stand on which were a pot of pulcho and two cups, hurried out. Kov Lutas filled the cups, and handing one to Thorne raised the other. "May we die like brave soldiers."

Thorne joined him. "It is a strange toast. Why do you speak of death?"

"Because it is so near. To be appointed as guards to the Dixtar's daughter is equivalent to a death sentence."

"I don't see why," Thorne replied. "Certainly every man who guards her isn't going to be so foolish as to lose his head over her."

"To 'lose his head' is indeed an apt expression. More than a hundred have already lost their heads, even as those two we saw this afternoon. Neva is said to be a heartless flirt, bent on conquest. Her father wants her to marry Sel Han, but she will not have him. And it is said that she flirts with every eligible male who crosses her path, just to spite them both. She is reputed to be irresistible, and her guards, of course, can't run away from her. Nor dare they affect to despise her advances, for her anger is fully as terrible as that of her father."

At this juncture an officer entered and saluted. "Which of you is Kov Lutas?"

"I am," replied the young Jen, returning his salute.

"If you are ready you will come with me to relieve the temporary guard of the Dixtar's daughter."

"I am ready," Kov Lutas told him. "Let us go."

They went out, and Thorne, after pouring himself another cup of pulcho, sat down to reflect on the situation. But he had scarcely settled in his swinging chair when Vorz came to the door and announced, "Salute the Deputy Dixtar."

Thorne sprang to his feet and raised his hand smartly in salute. Then he let it fall to his side as he recognized Sel Han.

"Greetings, Sheb Takkor Jen," said the Deputy Dixtar with a grin. "You seem surprised at seeing me."

"And to you, greetings, Sel Han," replied Thorne coolly. "To what do I owe the—er—honor of this unexpected call?"

Without replying, Sel Han walked to the taboret and helped himself to a cup of pulcho. Then he seated himself in Kov Lutas's chair. For a time, he sat there in silence, then spoke suddenly in English. "Shut the door."

Thorne closed the door and returned to his chair.

Sel Han nodded. "I thought so. Understands English."

"Perhaps when you have finished talking to yourself, you will explain your business," Thorne said.

"Don't get stuffy with me. I can put you on the spot, or I can make things good for you. I came to make you a proposition. What do you say, Harry Thorne?"

"I say you're wasting your time, Frank Boyd."

"Ah—I figured you knew. Well, I heard about your run-in with Sur Det. Pretty handy with a sword, aren't you? There wasn't another man in this country who could have made a monkey out of Sur Det the way you did.

"He was my teacher when I came here. I saw I needed to be handy with a sword, so I picked the best teacher I could find. Since I'm younger, faster, and have a longer reach, I got so I could beat him. Then I went and started to cut my way to the top. And I'm pretty close to it now."

"Did you come to entertain me with this modest little sketch?"

"No, I came to get a line on you—and give you a break if you're willing to play ball. I can cut you in on something big."

"Such as what?"

"I'd be talking out of turn if I told you. First, you do what I want you to do, then I'll make things right for you."

"I don't think we can talk business, Mr. Boyd."

"Don't be an idiot. Get this—you're taking orders, I'm giving them. Now this girl Neva is supposed to marry me, but she doesn't see it yet. Right now, just to spite her father and me, she's flirting with every man she meets. She'll probably make a pass at you. If you don't play, she'll send you to the mines—if you do, her father will have your head. You're on the spot unless you listen to me.

"What burns me now is that she won't even talk to me—calls the guard and has me thrown out every time I drop in to see her. Now here's all I want you to do. I'm going to drop in to see her tonight before I fly to Takkor. She'll probably want you to throw me out. If she does, tell her you can't in honor lay a hand on me, because I won that duel from you at the military school. That will let you out."

At this moment the door opened and an orderly entered with Thorne's evening meal. As he arranged the dishes on the taboret he noticed Sel Han.

"May I get the Deputy Dixtar something to eat?" he asked.

"No, I'm dining with the Dixtar," replied Sel Han, rising. He swung on Thorne. "Don't forget I'm not asking you, I'm telling you—and you'd better come through."

Without replying or looking up, Thorne drew his jeweled dagger and turned his attention to the food on the taboret which the orderly had set before him. A moment later he heard Sel Han leave the room.

Soon after he finished his meal, an officer came in and saluted.

"It is time for you to relieve Kov Lutas in the apartments of the Dixtar's daughter," he said.

CHAPTER 10

When Thorne, escorted by the palace officer, reached the apartments of Neva, the sun had set, and the luxuriously furnished rooms were lighted by the soft amber radiance of the half-hooded baridium globes which hung from the ceiling on golden chains. The size and magnificence of the suite reserved for the daughter of this apostle of simplicity who would make all citizens equal, was astounding.

The chamber in which he found himself opened onto a broad terrace which led to a private garden, separated from the rest of the palace grounds by a high wall. Kov Lutas, standing in the circular doorway, smiled at their approach.

"Greetings, Sheb Takkor," he said, after exchanging salutes with the two officers. "She whom we guard is resting on the terrace. The orders are to stay always within sight and call, and when she sleeps to stand guard just outside her chamber door."

Thorne took up Kov Lutas's position in the doorway. "I'll try to carry out orders. A good dinner and a sound rest to you."

"And to you a pleasant vigil," replied Kov Lutas.

Not until both officers had gone out did Thorne steal a glance at the girl he was to guard. He was unable to suppress a gasp.

Her eyes, languorous beneath the fringed curtains of their sleepy lids, were liquid pools of lapis lazuli. Her small nose was a most exquisitely chiseled bit of sculpture. Her red lips, sightly parted, revealed teeth that were matched pearls. And her hair was spun gold and sunbeams.

For some time she was motionless, gazing pensively out over the garden. Presently she crossed the terrace and descended to the garden. Watching her, Thorne stood bemused, wondering if it were possible that the scrawny, rat-faced Dixtar could be the father of so beautiful a daughter.

So potent was the spell cast over his senses that he lost sight of her in the shrubbery before he remembered his orders, and ran down the steps into the garden.

For some time Thorne hurried blindly about in the garden. Then the nearer moon, suddenly blinking above the rooftops to the west, came to his assistance. By its pale light he saw Neva not fifty feet from him, seated on the rim of a limpid pool in the center of which a fountain babbled.

Slowly he moved closer and halted at a distance of about twenty feet. As he stood there he was recalled to mundane considerations by a burning sensation in the region of his knees. Lowering his hand to investigate the cause, he discovered that heat rays were emanating from an ornate globe about two feet high which stood beside the path.

He had seen many such globes at various points around the garden and on the terrace. Although it had not occurred to him to wonder why the garden had not grown cold after nightfall, he now understood the reason.

In order to escape the discomfort caused by the proximity of the heating globe, he moved a few steps nearer the fountain. A dry twig snapped beneath his foot, and the girl looked up, a startled expression on her face.

"Have no fear," said Thorne. "I am Sheb Takkor, your new guard."

"I know," she replied. "It was the noise that startled me. You see, I am expecting some one I am not at all anxious to meet."

Though he felt quite sure he knew who that some one was, Thorne did not venture to say so.

Heavy footsteps sounded on the garden path. A shadow fell athwart the pool. Thorne glanced across to where the shadow began. Behind Neva stood Sel Han. "The Dixtar's deputy salutes his fair daughter," he said.

Without replying or even turning her head, Neva called to Thorne, "A trespasser has intruded upon my privacy, guardsman. Remove him."

The Earthman strode forward and stood facing his enemy. "It seems you are not wanted," he said quietly. "I trust that, under the circumstances, you will not have the bad taste to remain."

Sel Han laughed contemptuously. "Out of my way, worm," he ordered. "You dare not raise a hand against me." He sat down familiarly beside Neva. "Your guardsman is a spineless coward. Once he faced me, sword in hand, but grew so frightened before a blow had been struck that he dropped his weapon and fainted."

Thorne ground his teeth in impotent rage. He knew that under the Martian code he must suffer in silence any abuse which this fellow might choose to heap on him, physical violence or an assault with a weapon excepted.

"I would have you know, Sheb Takkor," Neva said, ignoring the presence of Sel Han, "that *all* the details of that unfortunate affair of yours at the training school are known to me. It was cowardly of your opponent to slash you when you were weakened from loss of blood and numbed by the virus of a desert blood-fly. And in full accord with that craven blow is his present refusal to again meet you, while he relies on the passivity which his technical victory imposes on you."

At this, the deputy forced a derisive laugh.

"Would it please the Dixtar's daughter to have her guard slain before her eyes?"

"It would please her guard," retorted Thorne, "to have the opportunity of defending himself."

"No doubt it would," grinned Sel Han. He moved closer to Neva. "Come," he said, "send away this cowardly guard who is powerless to help you. There is something I want to ask you."

Familiarly he passed his arm around her shoulders. And when, with blazing eyes, she would have leaped away from him, he held her tightly.

Thorne instantly whipped out his sword. "Release her or die," he commanded, presenting his point at the deputy's breast.

The deputy let her go, and stood erect, glaring. "Have you abandoned your honor?"

"I might ask you the same," retorted Thorne, sheathing his sword, "but I know a man is incapable of abandoning that which he has never had."

"It seems," said Sel Han, a deadly glitter in his eyes, "that you have forgotten the code—and something else."

"I am glad you have not forgotten that you are my guardsman, Sheb Takkor Jen," interposed Neva. "And since you are acting in that capacity, and not in your own personal interests, it would seem that you are at liberty to treat this trespasser as you would any other."

"I had hoped that the Dixtar's daughter would confirm me in that belief," relied Thorne. The Earthman's fist shot up in a short arc that ended beneath Sel Han's protruding chin. There was a tremendous splash as the deputy measured his length in the chilly pool.

Thorne leaped back and waited tensely, hand on hilt. His enemy came up sputtering and cursing luridly in English, then stepped over the rim. He bowed low before the girl.

"Permit me to congratulate the Dixtar's daughter on the singular efficiency of her guardsman. It is only exceeded by his total lack of honor."

Then he turned, and strode away with water sloshing in his boots and dripping from his clothing.

Thorne's hand fell limply from his sword hilt. He was bitterly disappointed, for he had felt certain that Sel Han would come out of that enforced bath raging and eager to try conclusions with him.

"The coward! The miserable, slinking coward!"

Neva was speaking, half to herself, as she gazed after the departing figure. She turned and looked up at Thorne.

"He is afraid to measure swords with you," she said, "but he will find some other way to be rid of you. He is cunning, oh, so cunning, and treacherous." She laid a slim hand on the Earthman's arm. "The deputy has considerable influence with the Dixtar, my father—but for that matter, so have I. And I will help you."

In spite of his preconceived dislike of this little beauty, Thorne thrilled at her glance and touch.

"I am honored that the Dixtar's daughter should be interested in preserving my worthless life," he replied.

"He is a strange and terrible creature, this Sel Han," she went on. "Did you notice the queer gibberish he used when he came up out of the water? Some incantation, perhaps, to a strange god. No doubt he is a sorcerer."

Recalling the deputy's lurid English curses, Thorne smiled to himself as he replied, "I doubt not that he was calling down the wrath of some deity on my head."

Neva yawned prettily. "I am sleepy," she said. "We will go in now, for I must retire. You may walk beside me."

Slowly, side by side, stepping in perfect unison, they went up the path which led to the house.

At the steps which led up to the terrace she took his arm. Again he felt the thrill of her touch, and fought it with every ounce of will power at his command.

As they entered the doorway a slave girl hurried up to take her mistress's cloak. Another moved the lever which uncapped the baridium light globes, making the room brilliant as day. And still another hurried in, bearing a tray on which was a tiny jeweled cup of steaming pulcho which she proffered to Neva.

"Bring another for the Jen," she said.

The girl hurried out, and returned a moment later with a larger cup.

"I drink to my brave and efficient guardsman," smiled Neva.

"And I to the lovely and precious jewel which he guards," replied Thorne.

CHAPTER 11

During the early watches of the night, Thorne, standing guard before Neva's chamber door, reviewed the doings of the day. Before seeing the Dixtar's daughter he had been firmly of the opinion that he loved Thaine. And he had resolved not to be overcome by the reputedly irresistible charms of Neva. But now her image was ever before him.

As he stood there, inwardly perturbed by his strangely conflicting emotions, he suddenly sensed that all was not as it should be—that some sinister, alien presence was quietly watching him.

Before retiring, one of the slave girls had pulled the levers which hooded all of the larger baridium globes, leaving only one tiny light uncovered. It shed a pale golden twilight that faintly revealed the outlines of the objects in the room.

Over all these objects Thorne's eyes now roved, yet he could discern nothing amiss. The swinging chairs and divans, depending from the ceiling by their golden chains, were obviously unoccupied. And the shadows beneath them were not so dense as to form a hiding place for a human being. There was a tall, shelved case in which many metal cylinders were kept, containing the scrolls which on Mars answered for books. But nothing could hide there. And other than these, there were only a few large pots of flowers set here and there about the room.

Once more he settled to his former position, but this time he only pretended to be preoccupied. For some time nothing happened, yet though his face was held straight ahead, he kept his eyes turned in the direction where he thought he had seen a stealthy movement. Suddenly, he saw it again. And to his astonishment, he discovered that it was a large pot of flowers which had moved. So far as he could see this pot and its contents were not markedly different from any of the others. It was about three and a half feet high and three in diameter at its center. And the two large handles projecting from its sides were of the same angular pattern as the others.

Without moving his head, he kept his eyes on this singularly mobile pot. Inch by inch it came toward him while he watched, fascinated. As it drew closer he examined it minutely, meanwhile stealthily loosening his sword in its sheath with his left hand. It seemed filled almost to the brim with rich black soil, from which the flower stalks projected.

Closer and closer it came until but a scant five feet separated them. Then it suddenly stood erect on two spindly legs and its handles turned into two spidery arms, one of which wielded a long, slim dagger. Straight for the Earthman it sprang, its weapon poised. But in that instant he had whipped his sword from its sheath, and whirling it over his head, brought it down with all his might on the amazing pot.

The hard vitreous shoulder of the pot withstood the blow of his slender weapon with ease, but the keen blade glanced downward, shearing off the spidery arm that held the dagger. At this there was a muffled shriek of pain from inside the pot, and turning, it fled swiftly for the doorway. As he set out in pursuit, Thorne shifted his sword to his left hand, and plucking his heavy mace from his belt, hurled it straight at the center of the pot.

The weapon went true to the mark. There was a resounding crash of broken crockery, and the spindle legs collapsed, precipitating everything onto the floor. Out of the tangle of crumpled flowers there rolled a round-bodied yellow man.

For some time pandemonium held sway in that quarter of the palace. Neva's frightened girls and women screamed for help, and a company of guards from the outer corridors came clanking into the room. But Neva herself, clad in a filmy wrap, came out of her sleeping room, quite unperturbed.

"What has happened, Sheb Takkor Jen?" she asked.

"That attacked me," Thorne replied, indicating the corpse, "disguised as a pot of flowers."

By this time the room was filled with soldiers and slave girls, all staring curiously at the remains. Some one had unhooded the baridium globe, and the resulting light revealed every detail.

The yellow man's disguise had been well adapted to his rotund body and spidery arms. The pot had a false bottom only two inches from the top, covered with a thin layer of soil. The flower stalks were set on narrow spikes projecting upward from this bottom. There were no handles, but holes through which the scrawny arms were thrust. Painted to resemble crockery and held akimbo, they had looked exactly like handles in the dim light. And the pot, with small holes bored in it for breathing and spying, formed an efficient body armor against sword and dagger thrusts.

"A diabolical attempt," said Neva, shuddering. Then to the soldiers, "Take it away."

Two men caught up the stiffening body and others cleared away the debris. Then, at a sign from Neva, all silently left the apartment.

She looked up into Thorne's eyes.

"You have saved me from abduction, or perhaps assassination," she said. "I am very grateful."

"Perhaps," he replied, "it is only myself I have saved. The fellow attacked me. And I have reason to believe he was the creature of Sel Han."

"What reason?"

"Because the Deputy Dixtar is said to be in league with the Ma Gongi."

"There may be some truth in that," she answered, "but don't let anyone hear you say it. My father has unlimited faith in his deputy, and has beheaded two officers who were bold enough to accuse him of that very thing."

"I am grateful for your warning," Thorne replied, "and will be discreet."

A slave girl drew back the curtain, and she reentered her sleeping room.

Morning found the Earthman exceedingly weary after a strenuous day and night without rest. Soon after he was relieved by Kov Lutas he was sound asleep in their apartment. It seemed that he had scarcely closed his eyes when the orderly awakened him.

"Your servant is commanded to prepare you to attend the Dixtar's daughter at the state function this evening," he said. "As the preparation will take some time, I was compelled to awaken you early."

CHAPTER 12

Like most of the women Thorne had known on his own world, Neva was a long time about dressing. But when, after he had waited for more than an hour before her door, she came forth, the result was most entrancing.

A tiara of pearls and pale blue amethysts woven together in a bizarre pattern on the meshwork of golden wires, bound her sun-bright hair. Beads of the same materials formed her breast-shields and supported a clinging bodice of iridescent blue silk. This vanished in a girdle of pearls and amethysts.

Thorne stood enthralled, and she smiled archly. Then she raised her arms and circled gracefully on the tips of her toes. "Like it?" she asked.

"Immensely," he replied, "even as I adore—" He stopped suddenly.

"Go on," she urged him, still smiling.

"Sorry. I said more than I intended. Perhaps you will find it in your heart to overlook my presumption."

"Perhaps I shall if you will finish." Then, "Even as I adore—" she prompted him.

"—the star-strewn firmament," he replied.

She stamped a tiny foot. "Must I command you?" She moved closer—laid a hand on his arm. "Where I might command," she said, "I will only implore."

"—the lovely jewel it adorns," he finished.

"Ah! That is what I wanted to hear you say. And now for your reward you will escort me to the reception as a gentleman and officer of the Kamud, walking at my side."

The reception of Irintz Tel, Dixtar of Xancibar, was a gorgeous affair. Held for the purpose of welcoming Lori Thool, the new ambassador from Kalsivar, largest and most powerful nation of Mars, it was a model of magnificence.

The function was held in the great central audience chamber of the palace, the ceiling of which towered a thousand feet above the heads of the assembled guests, its polished surface reflecting the rays of myriads of baridium globes, which made the place light as day.

Irintz Tel was standing with his illustrious guest on a dais in the center of the floor, presenting other visiting dignitaries and his chief officers, when the silvery notes of a trumpet rose above the hum of conversation. Instantly, every voice was hushed as a pompous major-domo announced: "The Dixtar's daughter."

All eyes were turned toward the doorway as Neva entered, walking beside Thorne. And though they lighted with pleasure at sight of the dainty little golden-haired beauty who was the first lady of Xancibar, not a few admiring glances were cast at the tall, handsome, sun-bronzed young officer.

Straight to the dais they went, the girl nodding to right and left to her many friends and acquaintances. As the little rat-faced Dixtar advanced to meet them, accompanied by Lori Thool, Thorne was once more struck by the incongruous dissimilarity between father and daughter.

The ambassador was tall, slender, and slightly under middle age, his hair just beginning to gray at the temples. He was quite handsome and elegant in his uniform and insignia of a great noble of Kalsivar.

"Neva," squeaked the Dixtar in his high-pitched voice, "this is Lori Thool, the noble ambassador from Kalsivar. Lori Thool, my daughter."

The ambassador saluted gracefully. "My homage to the most beautiful of the daughters of Mars. It must be that I have now met every one. Will you not join me in a game of gapun? I see they are setting up the boards."

"In a moment," she answered. "You have not quite met every one. This is my friend, Sheb Takkor Jen."

As he and the resplendent ambassador exchanged dignified salutes, the Earthman exulted over the fact that she had said, "my friend."

Meanwhile, Neva had beckoned a pretty little black-haired, brown-eyed beauty to her side.

"I take it that you have met the ambassador, Trixana," she said, "but not my friend, Sheb Takkor Jen."

Thorne acknowledged with a courtly salute, and a moment later found himself walking at the side of the vivacious little brunette, following Neva and Lori Thool as they made their way toward the gaming boards. From the corner of his eye, he saw Irintz Tel standing, chin on chest and hands clasped behind him. And he was quite positive that the Dixtar's look was not friendly.

A moment later he saw Sel Han slip up beside Irintz Tel and, bending, whisper some secret communication. The Dixtar nodded, and again flashed a look at Thorne.

Lori Thool and the two girls chanced much gold at the gaming boards, and Trixana won quite heavily. But Thorne only looked on. As he was standing, watching the game, he felt a touch on his arm, and turning, beheld the kindly face of the white-haired Lal Vak.

"Greetings, Sheb Takkor Jen," he said softly. "Turn and watch the game, while I deliver a message. We must not seem to be talking together."

Thorne looked back at the players, and the scientist continued: "You are in great danger. Sel Han is plotting against your life. He has denounced you to the Dixtar as being over-friendly with Neva, and her actions tonight in treating you as an equal have seemed to confirm his words. A friend has brought me news that Irintz Tel has just promised Sel Han he will turn you over to the headsman in the morning."

"What can I do about it?"

"Escape. Get away from the palace before morning."

"That I had already planned."

"How?"

"Over the garden wall."

"Splendid! It is just what we had in mind. I will have a conveyance waiting for you. Be there just after the farther moon rises and it may be that we can save you. Farewell."

When the gathering broke up, Lori Thool, after saying a lingering farewell to Neva, departed with his suite. Trixana was claimed by her father, a tall, handsome soldier in the prime of life, and Neva, left once more with Thorne, started toward the door. They had only gone a few steps when Sel Han suddenly strode up. He made a sweeping bow before Neva.

"May I have the honor of seeing the Dixtar's daughter safely to her apartments?" he asked.

She took Thorne's arm. "The Dixtar's daughter is adequately escorted."

Sel Han continued to bar her way, smiling cynically. And the Earthman noticed that the Dixtar himself was only a few feet away, looking on.

"Apparently you have not observed that the Dixtar's daughter wishes to pass," said Thorne. "Under such circumstances it should not be necessary to request any *gentleman* to stand aside."

At this, the deputy flashed a look at the Dixtar, as much as to say, "I told you so," and moved out of the way.

Back in the apartments of Neva, as Thorne stood guard before her chamber door, his mind was a mass of conflicting emotions. The time slipped by until he suddenly realized that the farther moon had risen and the hour had struck for his departure. He was about to steal softly away from his post when he was startled by a touch on his arm and a whispered, "Quiet."

Swiftly turning, he was astonished to see Neva standing there before the curtain clad in a filmy sleeping garment.

"Make no noise," she said, "and come with me. I heard someone on my balcony, and want you to surprise the prowler."

Softly they entered the sleeping chamber. For a moment Thorne stood there, accustoming his eyes to the dim light and taking note of his surroundings. Then he silently drew his sword and advanced toward the balcony, listening intently.

Reaching a window without having heard a sound, he cautiously leaned forward and peered out. So far as he could see, the balcony was deserted. He stepped out and explored. Still no sign of a prowler. Then he reentered the room.

"Did you see him?" she asked.

"I saw no one," he replied. "Perhaps you were only dreaming."

"No, no! I am positive a man was there a moment ago. Not only did I hear him, but I saw his shadow as the moon came up. I'm terribly frightened."

They were standing very close together. Her eyes, looking up into his, were wide with fear. She swayed toward him. Solicitously he threw his arms about her—felt that she was trembling. Her arms stole about his neck and clung. "Hold me tight—tight! In your arms I am not afraid."

Now it was the man who trembled; but not with fear. Their lips met.

"I love you, love you, love you!" she murmured. "Say again what you said to me this evening."

"I love and adore you," he told her, his voice husky with emotion. "Yet it is madness—a sweet madness."

"Why, dear one?"

"Because tomorrow . . ."

Suddenly the lights flashed on, and he paused, speechless with surprise.

A dozen armed soldiers rushed into the room, bared blades in their hands. At their head was Sel Han, a grin of triumph on his features. And behind them came Irintz Tel, Dixtar of Xancibar.

"Help! The guard! Release me, you brute!"

For a moment Thorne was in a daze. Then he suddenly realized that it was Neva who was speaking—that she was beating upon his breast with her clenched hands—hands that had caressed him but a moment before—straining to break from his clasp.

Mechanically he let her go. She ran to the little wizened Dixtar, buried her face in his shoulder, and began sobbing bitterly.

Thorne suddenly came to the full realization of his peril. He whipped out his sword and dagger and leaped for the door. Two warriors barred his progress.

A feint, a thrust, and one went down stabbed through the heart. He parried the thrust of the other with his dagger. Then he withdrew his blade from the heart of the first enemy and sheathed it in the throat of the second.

Other warriors leaped in close, but he bounded over the bodies of his two fallen adversaries and out of the door. Straight across the terrace he dashed, then down the steps and into the labyrinth of garden paths.

A few moments more and Thorne had reached his objective—a tall sebolis tree standing near the wall, which he had previously marked for his purpose. Pausing only to hurl his sword and dagger into the faces of his pursuers, he scrambled up the rough tree trunk, then climbed from branch to branch until he was above the level of the wall.

Walking out on the swaying branch until it sagged dangerously, he leaped. His fingers caught the edge of the wall, but it was rounded by a thousand years of weathering, and slippery with the night's accumulation of hoar frost.

With a last despairing clutch at the curved, treacherous surface, he fell to the ground twenty feet below.

As soon as he struck, a half dozen soldiers pounced on him. Weaponless, he fought them with fists and feet until Sel Han reached over and struck him on the head with the flat of his heavy mace. Then his captors, at a sharp command from the triumphant deputy, jerked him to his feet and half carried, half dragged him back to the palace.

Neva, attended by two of her slave girls, sat on a divan with a fluffy wrap around her shoulders. Irintz Tel was pacing up and down, chin on chest, hands clasped behind his back, his brow contracted in a frown and his thin lips compressed in a tight line.

Presently a tall, sad-faced man bearing a great, two-handed sword on his shoulder, strode into the room. Behind him walked a sleepy-eyed, frightened little boy who carried a basket.

"Strike the head from this despicable traitor, Lurgo," squeaked Irintz Tel, without looking up.

Lurgo the headsman lowered his huge weapon and stood leaning on the pommel, waiting while two warriors dragged Thorne to the center of the floor and forced him to kneel. Then he stepped back, carefully measured the distance with his practiced eye, and whirled the great blade over his head.

CHAPTER 13

"No, no! Lurgo! Wait!"

It was Neva who had sprung from her couch, and now stood between the sad-faced headsman and the kneeling Thorne.

Lurgo stared sorrowfully down at her, his blade still poised in mid-air.

Irintz Tel ceased his pacing for the first time and looked up. "What's this, daughter? Can it be that you care for this vile miscreant?"

"Care for him!" Neva stamped her foot angrily. "I hate him for the affront he has put upon me. For much less than this, you have caused minor offenders to suffer for days before death was finally granted them. Yet this seducer, this ravisher who has dared to lay hands on your own daughter is let off with a mere stroke of the headsman's sword. Do you hold my honor so lightly as this?"

"By the wrath of Deza, you are right!" exclaimed Irintz Tel. "I have been too hasty. Let be, Lurgo."

At this, the tall headsman sadly shouldered his sword and trudged away, the sleepy-eyed boy with the basket trailing in his wake.

"Does it not seem fair, my father," said Neva, "that since the crime of this malefactor was against me, I should be the one to pronounce sentence upon him?"

"It does indeed, daughter. It does indeed," agreed Irintz Tel. "Suppose you name his fate."

"Why, then, I'll sentence him to labor in the baridium mines," she said. "I hear that men are long in dying there, and that they suffer much."

"But," interposed Sel Han, "there are tortures . . ."

"Since when," asked Neva, facing him haughtily, "has the Dixtar's deputy acquired the right to question the mandates of the Dixtar's daughter?"

"You are right, daughter, you are right," interposed Irintz Tel. "You must not interfere, Sel Han. She has pronounced a fitting sentence, and we confirm it. Away with him, warriors."

Thorne, still dazed by the blow on his head, dimly comprehended that he had been saved from the stroke of the sworder only to be condemned to a worse fate.

As he was dragged away by the warriors, he saw the face of Irintz Tel sneering, that of Sel Han grinning malevolently, and those of the warriors stern and pitiless. But at Neva he did not look.

After conducting him through numerous passageways, the soldiers led him into a small room at one end of which a hole about three feet in diameter was cut in the wall. Into this hole they thrust him feet first, attached a tag to his arm marked "Baridium Mines," and gave him a violent push. With a speed that gave him a peculiar sensation in the pit of his stomach and caused a considerable pressure on his eardrums, he shot downward in a dark, slanting tube, the inner surface of which was as smooth as glass. Presently he glided over a series of rises which slowed his progress, then out into an open trough under a long, low shed. At the end of the trough two soldiers caught him and stood him erect.

To his surprise, Thorne now saw that he was in one of the large warehouses which lined the banks of the canal over which he had passed. After the soldiers had examined his tag he was herded with a group of other prisoners, similarly tagged, who were huddled around a large globe-heater on the dock. Here he stood, slowly turning like the others, for while the side toward the heater was comfortably warm, the one directly away from it was subjected to the freezing temperature of the early morning air.

Presently the sun, heralded only by a brief dawn-light in this tenuous atmosphere, popped above the horizon, its blue-white shafts instantly dissipating the cold, and swiftly melting the shell of ice which covered the canal.

Moored at the dock was a low, narrow craft about two hundred feet in length. The hull was of brown metal, and the upper structure was roofed over with iridescent, amber colored crystal curved like the back of a whale.

Through one of the doors the prisoners were now driven. As he followed along with the others, Thorne noticed the strange propulsive devices used on these craft, which were shaped much like the webbed feet and legs of aquatic birds, and were fastened at intervals along the sides.

As soon as the prisoners had been herded on board, the metal door clanged shut behind them. Shortly thereafter the craft glided away from the dock, propelled smoothly and noiselessly by its artificial webbed feet.

Thorne presently tired of the sameness of the scenery and entered into a conversation with one of his fellow unfortunates—a man who had once been high in the councils of the Kamud, but who had dared to oppose Irintz Tel. Levri Thomel was a silver-haired man in the late autumn of life. He showed no rancor against the Dixtar, but took his sentence as the decree of fate.

"At most," he told Thorne, "I would have only enjoyed a few short years of life. But you are a young man. Your case is sad, indeed, as you would have had much to live for."

For a time silence fell between them. Then Thorne asked, "What are these baridium mines like? Have you any idea?"

"There are vast workings, which require much machinery and equipment, and the labor of many slaves. The baridium ore, after being brought up from deposits far underground, is crushed and cleaned of all impurities. Then it is distilled. The liquid which passes over in the still is mixed with phosphorus and several other chemicals, and used to fill the light globes with which you are familiar. The solid residue left in the stills is calcined until it becomes an impalpable powder, fearfully water-hungry. Then it is combined with several elements, the most important of which is metallic sodium, to make the fire-powder which instantly ignites when moistened."

Thorne was about to ask him how all this affected the slaves, when the boat suddenly slowed down, then stopped beside a dock of black stone which jutted from the wall on the outer side of the canal. The metal door was thrown open, the prisoners were herded out and Thorne lost track of Levri Thomel.

They were marched through a high archway in the thick black wall, and thence into an immense building constructed of the same material. Here they formed in line, to be examined by an officer, who assigned them to various working groups. Thorne was pleased when he found that Levri Thomel was assigned to this group, which numbered about twenty men.

A guard marched them through a long corridor, lighted by small baridium globes, and thence into a broad courtyard which overlooked an immense pit, several miles in diameter, the rim of which was circled by a high black wall. As soon as they entered this court, the prisoners encountered air laden with fine dust and acrid fumes, which smarted their lungs and nostrils and set them to coughing and sneezing violently.

Meanwhile, the guard urged them onward to the edge of the pit, where he turned them over to another guard, whose face, head and body were protected by a breathing mask, helmet and air-tight suit.

This new guard spoke to them through a sound amplifier which projected from the top of his helmet.

"Down the stairway," he ordered, "and step lively. I'll make the first laggard regret his slothfulness."

The deeper they descended the more difficult breathing became, until, when they reached the bottom of the stairway, the fumes fairly seared their lungs, while the fine dust, settling on the skin, made them itch and burn. Merely being in the place without a protective suit was torment.

As these things came to Thorne's attention, he thought again of Neva. More sharply than the baridium fumes seared his lungs, the thought of her perfidy seared his heart.

CHAPTER 14

The group of slaves was ushered into a large building and set at the task of filling and sealing small phials of fire-powder. Here the laborers were seated at long benches, above which were suspended large hoppers of the powder. This was conveyed down to them by means of tubes with small valves at the bottom which could be opened or closed by the operator as the phials were filled.

Stoppers of red, resilient material like that which formed the suits of the guards were pressed into the bottles, then held for a moment against hot plates, the heat melting them down and sealing them hermetically.

The labor in this department was the lightest of any in the baridium pit. Yet it was the most dreaded of all, as the air was constantly filled with the searing powder which attacked skin and lungs alike.

With a sickening apprehension of the fate in store for him, Thorne gradually saw his own skin turning yellow from contact with the fumes and powder in the air. And despite the utmost watchfulness he was unable to avoid burning his fingers and the backs of his hands by spilling on them small quantities of powder which sifted down from the none too efficient valve.

When night came the slaves were herded into a great communal building, the only furniture of which consisted of heating globes. Here a coarse porridge was doled out to them. They were given water to drink.

In this building the air was somewhat freer from dust and fumes than outside, and therefore offered some slight relief to Thorne and other newcomers whose lungs and skin had not, as yet, been badly seared. After eating their rations, the slaves flung themselves down on the hard floor around the heating globes, many to fall asleep from utter exhaustion.

Thorne was about to fling himself down like the others when he saw, sprawled on the floor at his feet, a sleeping figure that somehow seemed familiar. The skin was yellow and mottled with many burns, yet he could not mistake Yirl Du, Jen of the Takkor Free Swordsmen.

Stooping, the Earthman shook his friend. Yirl Du's red-rimmed eyes blinked open. An angry snarl died in his throat as sudden recognition came to him. He sat up abruptly, saluted.

"I shield my eyes, my lord. I did not dream of seeing you here, and at first I did not recognize you with that yellow cast to your skin."

"You seem to have acquired considerable color yourself, old friend. How long have you been here?"

"The seven judges sentenced me the day you were taken before the Dixtar," Yirl Du told him. "The trial was a farce. There were no witnesses, and no evidence was produced against me except a letter from Sel Han."

Thorne made Yirl Du and the silvery-haired Levri Thomel acquainted, and for a time they conversed. Then the baridium globes which lighted the building here hooded, and they composed themselves for sleep.

It seemed, however, that he had scarcely fallen asleep when a small baridium hand-torch was flashed in his face, awakening him, and a guard prodded him with his foot.

"Are you Sheb Takkor?" the fellow asked in a hoarse whisper.

"I am," Thorne replied.

"Where is he who is called Yirl Du?"

"He sleeps here beside me."

"It seems you two have a powerful friend at Dukor. My superior officer has ordered me to assist you hence. Awaken Yirl Du and follow me."

The guard hooded his torch as Thorne shook Yirl Du awake and explained the situation to him. Then he thought of Levri Thomel. A touch awakened the old man.

"Come with me," Thorne whispered. "It may be that we can escape."

Then he called to the guard: "Ready."

The fellow opened the slide of his torch only wide enough to enable him to make his way among the sleeping slaves who sprawled on the floor. Then he started toward the nearest doorway, closely followed by Thorne, Yirl Du, and Levri Thomel. Once outside the building, the guard hooded his torch, and they made their way by the light of the nearer moon, which was dropping swiftly toward the eastern horizon. They presently came to a small guardhouse near the rim of the pit. Their conductor entered, and motioned them to follow.

Thorne marched in first, and found himself in the presence of an officer who sat on the edge of a swinging divan.

The officer looked up sharply. "What's this, Hendra Suhn? You have brought three of them."

The guard seemed dumfounded. "I only awakened Sheb Takkor, and told him to bring Yirl Du."

Thorne hastened to explain. "I am Sheb Takkor. These are my friends Yirl Du and Levri Thomel. It is my desire that both accompany me."

"I was only ordered to assist two, yourself and Yirl Du," said the officer. "Levri Thomel goes back."

"If he goes back, then I go with him," said Thorne.

"You refuse escape when it is offered you?"

"I decline to attempt it without my friend."

"The more fool, you," growled the officer. "Yet I have my orders to assist you, and I suppose this doddering old derelict must go with you." He arose, and stepping into another room brought two bundles of warm clothing, and two of weapons. One bundle of each he handed to Thorne and the like to Yirl Du. But Thorne instantly passed his bundles to Levri Thomel.

The officer glared for a moment, but checked himself, and went into the next room for more clothing and weapons, which he thrust into the hands of Thorne with ill grace.

"You win," he said angrily. "But this old wreck you persist in taking with you will yet cause your undoing."

Swiftly the three men donned the clothing and belted sword, mace and dagger about them. In addition to these, each was provided with a bundle of javelins in a quiver that hung by a strap across one shoulder.

"As soon as the nearer moon sets," said the officer, "and before the farther rises, you will have time to make your way in the dark up the side of the pit. The rim is guarded, but one guard has orders to pass you. That guard is stationed directly above this building. When you have passed the guard, you will proceed out into the desert until you have passed five out-cropping rocks. At the northern base of the sixth, which you will recognize because it leans as if it were about to fall to the ground, you will find supplies left there for you by your friends, because they would have been awkward for you to carry up the side of the pit."

"Who are these friends who have been so thoughtful?" asked Thorne.

"I only know that these orders came down to me from my superiors, and that they must have had them from some one high in the councils of the Kamud."

So swiftly did the nearer moon move across the sky, that only a short time elapsed ere it dropped below the eastern horizon. Then the three men set out.

Overhead, the stars were blazing jewels of white, red, pale blue and yellow, in a sky of jet. Though their combined radiance was too feeble to light the path of the three fugitives, they were still of service, for their line of disappearance marked the rim of the pit. And one constellation which Thorne fixed in his mind served as a guide to the point, directly above the house they had just quitted, where they expected to find a friendly guard.

Moving with great caution in order not to start a landslide on that steeply sloping bank, they began the ascent. It was a long, difficult climb, and they had scarcely reached the summit when the farther moon rose in the east close to the point where the nearer moon had vanished a short time before. Its light was more dim than that of the nearer and larger orb, but bright enough to reveal them to a tall guard who stood looking out over the pit. Instantly he raised a javelin and advanced threateningly.

"Who are you?" he demanded.

"Sheb Takkor and friends."

The guard stared at him suspiciously. "I can pass but two. The third must go back."

"That order was changed. You will pass three or none," Thorne told him. "We are going on at once. Raise an alarm now, and we will kill you. Raise it later, and there is one high in the councils of the Kamud who will see that you are condemned to the powder room."

"I crave pardon, Sheb Takkor Jen," he said humbly. "Pass, and may Deza guard you."

And so the three now clambered over the wall, dropped to the other side, and marched out into the desert, free men.

Carefully, now, they counted the outcropping stones of which the officer had told them. They had passed the fifth, at a considerable distance from the pit, and were just coming up to the sixth when a half dozen warriors suddenly broke from a nearby clump of conifers and charged toward them, hurling a cloud of javelins.

Thorne shouted a warning to his companions, both of whom were able to dodge the barbed weapons. He called to his two friends to support him on the right and left, then dashed straight at the advancing warriors.

There was another exchange of javelins, in which the skilled Yirl Du transfixed an enemy, cutting the attacking party down to five.

Both sides expended their store of javelins at about the same time. Then swords and daggers were drawn and the hand-to-hand fighting began. Thorne engaged the blade of the leader of the band, and was instantly beset by another warrior on the fellow's right. Over at his left, Yirl Du fought alone. Levri Thomel, on his right, was attacked by the remaining two, and showed amazing skill with sword and dagger.

For a time there was only the clash of steel on steel and an occasional grunt from one of the wounded contestants. Then Thorne thrust the leader of the band

67

through the throat. With his chief opponent out of the way it was but child's play for him to quickly dispose of the other. Then, seeing that Yirl Du was getting the best of his assailant, he dashed to the assistance of Levri Thomel.

The old man still stood his ground, apparently unhurt, as Thorne came in to engage one of his opponents. A clumsy fencer, the fellow quickly succumbed. At the same instant Levri Thomel ran his antagonist through the heart. Turning, Thorne saw Yirl Du coming toward them, cleansing his blade with a bit of fabric cut from the cloak of his fallen adversary.

"A glorious victory, my lord. Six enemies stretched out on the sand, and we three still live."

"It was well fought," agreed Thorne. "But who could these men be? And how came they to be waiting here for us?"

"I recognized the last fellow I killed," said Yirl Du. "He was a henchman of Sel Han. The spies of the deputy evidently discovered the plot to release us, and he posted these assassins here for the purpose of ambushing us. He expected but two, and we were three—enough to defeat his cutthroats and upset his scheme."

"That is true," agreed Thorne. He turned to Levri Thomel. "It is you, my friend, who turned the tide. But for you, Yirl Du and I would now be stark on the sand in the place of these six assassins. Until I am able to express my appreciation more fittingly, permit me to merely thank you."

"It is I who owe you a lasting debt of gratitude," protested the old man. "But for you I would be down there in the pit, doomed to a lingering death. As it is, I—I . . ." Suddenly he swayed, and pitched forward on his face.

Alarmed, Thorne sprang to his side, and, turning him over asked: "What is it, my friend? Are you ill?"

"Ill unto death," the old fellow replied. "I was wounded early in the engagement and have been bleeding freely since. It is the end I would have chosen. Farewell, my comrades."

Hastily, Thorne undid his cloak, exposing a wound just above the heart. For a moment he held his hand there, but felt no pulsations.

"Levri Thomel is dead," he solemnly told Yirl Du.

"He was a brave man, my lord. And now we must look for that leaning stone, and be gone. If the morning sun finds us near the baridium pit, we too are dead men."

Sadly, silently, they gathered their javelins and moved forward. Presently they came to the leaning stone.

"It was at the north base of the stone we were to look," said Thorne, "yet there is nothing here."

Yirl Du thrust a javelin into the sand. At a depth of about ten inches it encountered an obstruction. Swiftly he dropped to his knees and began scooping out the sand with his cupped hands.

CHAPTER 15

After a few moments of digging, Yirl Du grasped something and dragged it up out of the sand. It was a pole about eight feet in length, one end of which was inserted in a cylinder six inches in diameter and four feet long. Three pairs of straps were fastened to this cylinder and a bit of stirrup-shaped metal projected from its lower end.

At the opposite end of the pole was a cone-shaped cushion of reddish-brown resilient material.

Swiftly the Jen of the Takkor Free Swordsmen unearthed three more objects like the first, and two poles about sixteen feet long. Then he dragged out two large metal water bottles and two boxes, to all of which carry-straps were attached.

Opening one of the boxes, Thorne discovered food, fire-powder and medical supplies. Among these was a bottle of jembal gum. He heated some of this by burning a small quantity of fire-powder. Then he dressed Yirl Du's wounds and burns, after which his henchman did the like for him.

"Now, my lord," said Yirl Du, "if you will be seated I will strap on your desert legs for you."

Although Thorne had no idea what the pole and cylinder combinations were for, he began to understand when his retainer brought two of them and, after inserting his feet in the stirrups, began strapping them to his legs. When they were properly fastened in place, he next strapped a box to the Earthman's back, slung his javelins in their quiver, and hung his water bottle by a strap across his shoulder. Then he handed him one of the poles.

"Now you are ready, my lord," he said, "and I'll be on my own desert legs very shortly."

It did not take Yirl Du long to do for himself what he had done for Thorne. Then, grasping his pole with both hands, he thrust one end into the sand beside him, and drew himself up until he stood on his two long stilts. Thorne followed his example. With his weight on them the tops of the stilts were compressed a little way into the cylinders, which evidently contained powerful springs. The resilient, cone-shaped feet kept the stilts from sinking into the sand and added to the illusion of floating feather-like through space which the springs induced.

Yirl Du started off, walking toward the northwest. Thorne attempted to imitate his gait, but found it quite difficult, much like walking on bed springs or an aerial artist's net. At each step his desert legs threw him forward like a springboard, so that several times he was compelled to use his long pole to keep from falling on his face.

Presently he got the swing of it, whereupon Yirl Du gradually increased the pace until both of them were running. Not until then did the Earthman discover the tremendous advantage of traveling with desert legs. At each step the stilt now sank deeply into the cylinder, then hurled him upward and forward like a catapult.

The night was cold and frosty, and the exercise just sufficient to make him draw in great lungsful of the sweet desert air. What a relief after the baridium pit, with its searing, acrid fumes and its deadly clouds of corrosive dust!

As the night wore on and morning approached, the bright nearer moon once more popped above the western horizon, and hurtling forward to greet its slower, paler companion, made the sand particles and frost crystals glitter and sparkle. But long before the two moons could meet in the sky, the sun, heralded by a brief flash of silver-gray light, shot above the eastern horizon in the full blaze of its glory, and both satellites faded from view.

A few moments later, Yirl Du sighted a clump of conifers, and the two men made for it. They found a dry waterhole, but this did not daunt them with their full bottles, and the trees offered concealment and shade. Unstrapping their desert legs, they gathered firewood, brewed pulcho, and with the hot, stimulating beverage, washed down their morning meal of dried meat and hard traveler's cakes. Then, after extinguishing their fire with sand, they stretched out in the shade to sleep.

Thorne fell asleep almost immediately. Nor did he awaken until Yirl Du shook him soundly.

"The day is all but sped, my lord," he said. "I have brewed fresh pulcho and prepared our evening meal. We should eat and be ready to start as soon as the sun sets."

"What of our enemies? It seems strange that no signs of pursuit have developed."

"But they *have* developed," replied Yirl Du. "I am a light sleeper, and several times during the day as I lay awake, I saw bands of warriors mounted on gawrs flying overhead. Had they paused to search our hiding place we would have been killed or captured long ere this. Fortunately they did not."

The sun set just as they finished their meal, and they packed their belongings and strapped on their desert legs by the light of the nearer moon. Then they set out once more. Yirl Du had estimated that by traveling all night and sleeping during the daytime, they would be able to reach the edge of the Takkor Marsh in three nights. Here he would know how to find Thaine, if she were still alive and uncaptured, and they would be able to fulfill Thorne's promise to help her search for her father.

They made swift progress traveling by the light of the nearer moon, but it soon set and as on the night before there was a period of darkness during which only the stars and planets glittered overhead. This slowed them down considerably, as they were forced to proceed in the dark with extreme caution. And so, when the farther moon appeared above the eastern horizon, they welcomed it with joy, for it meant that they could set out once more at full speed.

They had traveled for some time by its pale light when Thorne noticed, over at his left, an object projecting above the horizon which he at first took for a tall, tufted conifer. But he suddenly became aware that it was moving; not like a tree swaying in the breeze, but actually traveling over the ground and coming with considerable speed in his direction. As the thing rapidly drew closer he was able to make out a huge head with a hooked beak, a long, scrawny neck, and a large, bird-like body supported by two legs, each of which was at least fifteen feet in length. The head of the monster, he judged, towered at least thirty feet above the ground.

He called to his companion. "Ho, Yirl Du. Do you see what is coming after us?"

His henchman looked around. "A koree! We must hasten, or we are dead men. It is the great man-eating bird of the desert."

They accelerated their pace from a trot to a run. Soon they had lengthened their thirty-foot steps to nearly fifty. But the koree kept coming on, and despite their utmost exertions, gaining on them.

Thorne, less skillful with the desert legs than his companion, began to fall behind, while the monster, still shortening the distance between them soon towered only fifty feet behind. It was a hideous thing—a giant bird with a crest of waving plumes, and a huge curved beak that looked fully capable of cutting a man in two with a single snap.

Its long lean neck was bare of feathers and covered with a wrinkled, leathery skin. Like the neck, the body was leathery and naked. The wings, which were short and obviously useless for flight, were featherless, but covered with sharp, horny protuberances which made them quite formidable weapons. The long legs were armored with large, rough scales, and the toes were equipped with sickle-shaped retractile claws. The monster ran with its ugly head projecting far forward and its wings sticking stiffly out from its leathery body, as if to prevent its intended victim from suddenly doubling back to the right or left.

In the meantime Yirl Du, noticing that the koree was likely to catch up with Thorne at any moment, dropped back beside him.

"We must separate," Yirl Du told him. "The bird will follow one of us. The other must then turn and follow it, hurling as many javelins into it as possible."

They separated, and the bird followed Thorne. Yirl Du instantly turned and pursued it. His first throw struck just behind the left wing, but despite his great strength and skill at hurling the javelin, he was only able to drive it through that tough skin for a little way. A second, striking below it, penetrated to a depth of about a foot. But it was enough to exasperate the monster, which turned and rushed at its persistent tormentor.

Thorne now turned and hurled a javelin. Striking at the point where the right leg joined the body it only penetrated deeply enough for the barb to hold. He tried a second cast, this time throwing with all his might. The javelin passed clear over the body of the bird and struck it in the back of the neck. Like the first, however, it only sank in up to the first barb, and therefore did not do much damage. It was enough, however, to make the monster turn and charge him.

Instantly the Earthman shot out at right angles to the course he had been following. But he made the mistake of watching the bird without looking at the ground before him, and ran straight into a tangle of desert sand-flowers. First one stilt, then the other, caught in the snarl of tough vines, and he plunged, face downward, into the sand about twenty feet beyond.

He managed to retain his grip on the long pole he carried, although it had been split when he fell, and now, after turning on his back, attempted to raise himself onto his desert legs once more.

But he was not quick enough. Already the koree towered above him, its huge beak distended for the kill.

CHAPTER 16

As the frightful head of the koree darted down to seize him, Thorne, lying where he had fallen, gripped his walking pole with both hands. Instinctively he struck at the descending horror with the pole.

The blow did the creature no injury, but it did distract the monster's attention from the man. Evidently taking the pole for a part of Thorne's anatomy, it seized it with the immense beak, and, bracing its feet like a robin drawing a worm from the ground, pulled upward.

Thorne, still clinging to the pole, was surprised to find himself standing on his desert legs once more, not three feet from the base of that leathery neck, which the bird had stretched to the utmost. Still clinging to the pole with his left hand, he whipped out his sword with his right. Then he slashed at that taut neck; the keen, saw-edged blade sheared through to the vertebral column.

As the blood spurted from the gaping wound, the Earthman let go of the pole and sprang away, almost colliding with Yirl Du, who had hurled all his remaining javelins in a fruitless effort to distract the monster's attention, and was now rushing in with drawn sword. The bird dropped the pole and plunged after them. But it had only taken a few steps when it collapsed and lay still.

Cautiously, the two men now approached the fallen giant. Yirl Du let himself to the ground, unstrapped his desert legs and set about gathering the javelins that still had sound shafts. This done, he recovered Thorne's walking pole for him. Then he donned his desert legs once more, and they resumed their journey.

Morning found them in a bleak section of the desert that was devoid of vegetation as far as they could see in every direction. As there was no fuel available, they washed their dry rations down with plain water instead of pulcho. Then they buried their desert legs, poles, boxes and bottles in the sand, dug other holes, and covered themselves until nothing showed but their transparent masks. Thus, protected from the sun as well as the prying eyes of any pursuers who might chance to fly over this spot, they slept.

As soon as the sun had set they had another cold meal and were off again. In the early hours before dawn, when the combined light of both moons made everything stand out clearly around them, they reached the top of a rugged cliff which somehow looked familiar to Thorne. Then he recalled that a line of such cliffs rimmed the ancient ocean bed in which the Takkor Marsh lay.

They paused on the brink and looked over. About a hundred feet below them was a broad ledge. At approximately the same distance below that was still another. And seventy feet farther down was the sloping, boulder-strewn beach.

Suddenly, to Thorne's consternation, Yirl Du deliberately stepped over the edge of the cliff. The Earthman uttered an exclamation of horror as he saw his henchman drop straight toward the ledge a hundred feet below. But Yirl Du alighted squarely on his desert legs, sank almost to the depth of the cylinders, and then shot forward and upward. Soaring over the rim of the ledge on which he stood, he dropped to the next, bounced onward again, and alighted on the ground below.

Thorne decided to risk the jump. Accordingly, he stepped over the edge of the cliff into empty air.

There was a vertical rush of wind past his face, then his stilts plunged almost to the tops of the cylinders, and he shot upward once more. As he had neglected to throw himself far enough forward he bounced twice before he got over the rim of the ledge. But when he next alighted he knew how to throw his weight to the front so he was catapulted over the rim. A moment later he joined Yirl Du, and together they scrambled down the sloping beach until they came to a zone of trees, vines and underbrush so thickly entangled that they made any further use of the desert legs impossible.

They let themselves to the ground, and removing these devices, hid them in the underbrush together with the poles, and continued their advance afoot.

The rising sun found them on the bank of a little stream at the edge of the marsh. Here they brewed pulcho and ate their morning meal. Then they flung themselves down for a short rest, lying so that the sun would awaken them by mid-morning.

Thorne awoke first. To his delight, he noticed that the yellow discoloration from the baridium fumes had entirely disappeared from Yirl Du's skin. He examined his own hands. They, too, had returned to their normal color. As he had no mirror in which to view his face, he went down to the stream.

He had knelt on the bank, and was just parting the rushes, when a reflection in the water before him made him look up. A huge black bat was pursuing what at first glance appeared to be a large butterfly. Apparently disabled, the smaller creature fluttered groundward, falling into the rushes not ten feet from Thorne.

In a steep spiral, the bat swooped toward its fallen prey. Leaping to his feet, Thorne saw the futile fluttering of a pair of lacy, opalescent wings above the rushes, and knew that in a moment more the bat would claim its victim. He jerked a javelin from his quiver and hurled it at the descending monster. It struck the black, furry neck with such force that the barbed head emerged from the other side.

Now it was the bat which tumbled into the rushes, only a few feet from the creature it had struck down.

Having satisfied himself that the ugly thing was dead, Thorne stepped over for a closer look at its intended prey. But as he did so, the lacy wings suddenly rose above the bushes, and he stifled a cry of amazement when he saw that they were attached to the shoulders of a slender, perfectly formed girl about three feet in height.

Save for a girdle of filmy, pale green material drawn tight at the waist by a belt of exquisitely wrought golden mesh and ending in a short skirt, she was nude. Her silky skin was a perfect flesh tint, and covered with a fine down, delicate as peach bloom. Her golden yellow hair was bound by a fillet of woven green jade links, circling her forehead just below two delicate, feathery antennae, which swept upward and backward like a pair of dainty plumes.

As he stood staring down at her, scarcely believing his eyes, she suddenly faded from his view.

The Earthman blinked and looked again. But where she had stood he now saw only the rushes which had been bent downward by the weight of her tiny body.

Faintly he heard the fluttering of wings overhead. He looked up and saw only the empty sky. Suddenly a little pixie voice, musical as a silver bell, broke the silence.

"I know you now, man of the Old Race," it said. "You are Sheb Takkor, the younger. You have saved the life of Eriné, daughter of the Vil of the Ulfi, and she is not ungrateful. Hold out your hand."

In obedient wonder, he extended his hand. A glittering something dropped into his palm. He saw that it was a tiny ring fashioned from platinum and set with a sparkling green gem.

"If you should ever need the Ulfi, rub the jewel and if there is an Ulf within scent of the ring he will be yours to command."

"Very kind of you," said Thorne, "but . . ." He suddenly realized that the fluttering had stopped. He was talking to empty air.

Yirl Du had come down the bank and was surveying him quizzically. "Your pardon, my lord. Were you speaking to me?"

"Yes. No. I was speaking to an Ulf—that is, to an Ulf maiden."

"Has one of the Little People paid us a visit?"

"Not intentionally, I guess. You see, she was struck down by that bat." Thorne indicated the carcass. "I saw her fall, thinking her only a butterfly, yet I pitied the creature and so slew the bat with a javelin. She became invisible and presented me with this." He held out the ring.

Yirl Du exclaimed with astonishment. "Why, that is indeed a precious thing, my lord, and such a gift as only the Vil of the Ulfi or a member of his family might present to a man."

"She named herself Eriné, daughter of the Vil."

Thorne was brimming over with questions about the Little People, but resolved to curb his curiosity until he could talk to Thaine or Lal Vak. Sheb Takkor, he reasoned, would be supposed to know these things. To question Yirl Du about them would be to make him suspect either that he was not Sheb Takkor, or that he had taken leave of his senses.

He kept silence while they climbed the bank to get their belongings. Thorne was about to strap his box to his back when Yirl Du said, "Wait. Let us first get our water-shoes."

"Water-shoes! I didn't see any in my box."

Yirl Du opened his box and took out a cylinder of rolled, reddish brown material. The Earthman then remembered having seen such a cylinder in his box, and extracted it. Unrolling it, he found it consisted of two hollow pieces of resilient material, to each of which was attached a small tube with a shut-off valve. He observed that Yirl Du had opened the valve on one of his and was inflating it by blowing through the tube, so he followed his example. Soon each had a pair of buoyant, boat-shaped water-shoes.

After adjusting their weapons and other paraphernalia, they carried the shoes down to the water's edge and donned them by pushing their toes under elastic bands designed to cross the arch of the foot. This done, they stepped out onto the surface of the stream.

Yirl Du started off downstream, moving with strokes much like those of a skater. Thorne, trying to imitate him, found that water-shoeing was more difficult than it looked. At the first attempt, his legs spread so far apart he came near to sitting down in midstream. Again and again he tried to glide forward as his henchman had done, but it always seemed that both feet were very definitely bent on traveling in different directions.

Observing his efforts, Yirl Du said, "I fear we should have rested longer, my lord. You have grown weak from your wounds."

"No, just out of practice," Thorne told him. "I didn't use any water-shoes while I was at school, you know. I'll get back the hang of it, presently."

And at length, by persistent effort, he did get the hang of it. By the time the sun had reached the zenith they were moving side by side in perfect unison, with long, rhythmic strokes. During this time they had traveled on a dozen winding streams, crossed six small lakes, and three times removed their water-shoes for short jaunts across the land.

At present they were gliding across the calm, mirror-like bosom of a lake much larger than any they had crossed thus far, when Thorne, chancing to notice a shadowy reflection in the placid water at his right, looked upward. To his alarm, he saw that a group of about twenty warriors, each mounted on a gawr, were gliding down toward them. And the warriors were mail-clad, round-bodied yellow men.

"Look, Yirl Du!" he cried, pointing aloft. "The Ma Gongi!"

His companion took one look. "Straight toward that point of land, quickly! It is our only hope."

They had been making for the mouth of a little stream, beside which the point of land projected. Now they turned almost at right angles to their course and made for the shore which was about two hundred yards distant.

But they had traveled only a few strokes toward their objective when a large net, hanging on four cables, was dropped by one of their pursuers. In an instant it had scooped up Yirl Du. Thorne saw him struggling futilely like some captured wild thing—saw him draw his dagger and vainly try to cut the metallic meshes.

Then the Earthman heard a swish in the water behind him, and he, too, was scooped up in a huge net.

CHAPTER 17

As soon as he felt the net swish under him in the water, Thorne instinctively dived forward in an effort to evade it. But it had traveled too far beneath him to make such an attempt successful. However, he was able to catch hold of the rim with both hands, and clung to this as he was borne aloft, so he did not sink into the toils as Yirl Du had done.

An instant later he was soaring fifty feet above the treetops, and though he well knew the risk he ran, decided on a desperate attempt at escape. Accordingly, he drew himself up until the edge of the net was on a level with his thighs, then turned a somersault and let go, falling feet foremost.

His feet were still thrust through the bands of his pneumatic water-shoes, and these helped, to a considerable extent, in breaking his fall as he crashed downward through the branches of a large tree. Straight down through the foliage he plunged, and upon striking the ground bounced upward like a rubber ball on his resilient water-shoes. After several gradually diminishing bounces, he checked himself by clutching a shrub. Then he swiftly removed the water-shoes, and, taking them under his arm, dashed away through the thick undergrowth.

So dense was the leafy tangle overhead that Thorne was unable to see his enemies, though he heard their shouts and learned that a warrior was landing. But this same dense canopy prevented his enemies from seeing him, and for this he was thankful.

He was grieved by the capture of his faithful retainer, but he could not possibly help Yirl Du, and would only render his own capture or death certain. Moreover, there was his debt to Thaine. Somehow he must contrive to escape for her sake.

It was not long before he came to a narrow stream, almost completely concealed from observers in the sky by the branches and lianas which arched and interlaced across it.

The stream, he soon found, had seemingly endless ramifications, and he traveled for several hours; in this manner he grew weary, hungry and thirsty, and decided to stop for rest and refreshment. Instead of sleeping directly out on the bank, he caught hold of a low-hanging liana, by means of this reached another, and swung himself up into a tree. Removing his water-shoes and slinging them over his back, he now traveled for some distance by swinging from tree to tree before alighting on the ground.

Wearily he flung himself down on a bed of soft moss beneath the spreading branches of an immense, aromatic sebolis tree. Then, after a pull at his water flask, he opened his box and removed therefrom a ration of dried meat and a cake. These he washed down with copious droughts of cold water. He rested there on the moss for a while, then packed up and wandered on.

As he felt that he had effectively baffled his pursuers, and knew that he was hopelessly lost, he saw no great need for haste. And so he wandered on through this strange Martian jungle, pausing at times to examine odd flowers or fruits, and marveling at its fantastic and often gigantic-insect life, as well as its many queer beasts, birds and reptiles.

Part of the time he walked on boggy land from which the water oozed at each step, and often he splashed through shallow pools. At other times he was compelled to don his water-shoes to cross flooded areas where the trees stood in the water.

There were also considerable stretches of high, dry land, usually quite heavily wooded.

Shortly after he had entered one of these he suddenly sighted a colony of pale green caterpillars, the bodies and heads of which were protected by sharp yellow spikes. There was a great diversity of size among them, the smallest being barely an inch in length, while the largest were more than three feet long and proportionately thick. All were browsing on leaves except a few of the largest individuals, which were busy spinning cocoons. He noticed many finished cocoons hanging from limbs by twisted, rope-like fastenings. They were pale green in color, and of a glistening, silky texture.

Presently he came to one hanging directly above his path, its lower tip at the height of his head. Curiously, he extended his hand to feel the silky covering, and pinched it to test its thickness. But scarcely had he done so ere a mournful, wailing cry smote his ears. It sounded much like the cry of a newborn human child, and seemed to come from the cocoon he had touched.

He jerked his hand away, but the wailing continued. Then he was suddenly aware of the whirring of a host of invisible wings in the air above him. There was a sharp twang, and a tiny arrow embedded itself in the ground at his feet. A second whizzed past his ear, and a third grazed his arm.

He realized that he was being attacked by the Little People, and suddenly thought of the ring. Snatching it from the pouch in which he had placed it, he rubbed it briskly on his palm. At this the twanging of the bowstrings ceased, and where he had only heard the beating of their wings, he now saw a number of Ulf men hovering in the air.

All of them were slightly larger than Eriné; there was as much diversity of appearance among them as there would have been in a similar sized group of humans. Their antennae were longer than those of the Ulf girl, and projected from shiny metal headpieces, notched at the front to let them through. They wore shirts of light chain-mail which reached to their thighs, drawn in at the middle by green silk belts from which depended swords and daggers. In addition to these weapons, each man carried a small bow in his hand, and a quiver of arrows strapped to his thigh.

One of the tiny warriors alighted on the ground, and advancing, saluted Thorne respectfully.

"Fleeswin, a Jen of the Ulf Archers, shields his eyes in the light of your presence, man of the Old Race and friend of Estabil, the Great One," he said. "We regret that we attacked you unknowingly, and humbly craving your pardon, place ourselves at your disposal and under your command."

"My greetings to you and your archers, Fleeswin Jen," Thorne answered, returning his salute. "Actuated by curiosity I touched this cocoon, not meaning to injure it."

"Our infants are easily frightened by the touch of strangers," Fleeswin said, "and we who guard them cannot watch them all at one time. We would lose many that might otherwise be saved if they did not summon us when menaced or interfered with."

"Then I am fortunate that your marksmanship was no better."

"Had you been one of the Ma Gongi, you would now be bristling with arrows," Fleeswin hastened to inform him. "But we saw you were of the Old Race, so only shot to drive you away. What would you with us, Bearer of the Ring?"

"If you can help me to find Thaine, daughter of Miradon Vil, I'll be grateful," Thorne answered. "I am the Rad of Takkor and her friend."

As soon as he had announced his title, every member of the little company saluted.

"We are doubly honored," said Fleeswin, "that you prove to be the Lord of Takkor as well as a Bearer of the Ring. As for finding Thaine, if she is anywhere within the Takkor Marsh, our Vil can find her for you. Permit me to conduct you to him."

After sending a warrior ahead to announce their coming, and placing another in temporary charge of the archers, Fleeswin led the way. Presently, above the drone of insects and the songs of birds, Thorne heard a haunting exquisite fantasy of sound which seemed to emanate from a carillon of no less than a thousand tiny silver-tongued bells. Yet he knew, as he drew closer, that it was not bells he heard but a chorus of Ulf voices. Soon he was able to distinguish the words of their song, and was surprised to learn that it was a paean of welcome for him.

A moment later he and Fleeswin emerged into a pleasant glen, the verdure-clothed sides of which rose steeply at his right and left. The place literally swarmed with the Ulfi, both male and female, and all were singing—some hanging suspended in the air with fanning wings, some perched in the trees or upon outcropping rocks on the hillside, some standing in cave mouths, with which the place was honeycombed, and others gathered on the mossy ground.

Fleeswin now kept to the ground, marching as if some great and honorable task had been delegated to him. As Thorne came abreast of the first singers, these began showering him with tiny, fragrant white blossoms. Then a group of two-score pretty Ulf maidens fluttered down and some draped Thorne with garlands while others strewed flowers before him.

Suddenly the music ceased, and Thorne, his body swathed with ropes of blossoms, found himself standing before a jovial looking pot-bellied old Ulf with a merry twinkle in his eyes. He sat enthroned on the lip of a large lily.

"Greetings, Sheb Takkor Rad," cried the little old fellow on the lily throne, returning his salute. "Estabil, Vil of the Ulfi, bids you welcome to Ulf-land, and desires to publicly thank you for saving the life of his precious daughter, Eriné. If there is aught that Estabil can do for you, you have but to make known your wishes."

"I wish to find . . ." Thorne began.

"I'll spare you the trouble of saying more," Estabil interrupted. "You wish to find Thaine. That we can promise to perform for you."

He leaped nimbly down from the lily throne, and continued: "Now that that is done, will you not stay to eat and drink with us?"

"Of course," Thorne assured him, "but it is important that I find Thaine, quickly. I should prefer to stay only long enough to drink a friendly cup with you, though if I were not pressed for time your hospitality would be most welcome. I'm sure you understand."

"We do. Indeed we do," Estabil replied. He turned and raised his hand, whereupon a little bearded Ulf struck a gong. Then there issued from the mouth of a cave in the hillside a figure Thorne instantly recognized. It was Eriné. Behind her came an Ulf maiden bearing a golden tray on which reposed three tiny platinum cups that sparkled with jewels, and a jar.

Thorne saluted as the Vil's daughter approached, and she smiled up at him.

"I hoped I might greet you at the banquet table," she said, "but since you cannot tarry with us, I bring you the cup of friendship and of farewell."

So saying, she filled the three jeweled cups from the jar, handed one to Thorne, one to her father, and retained one for herself.

81

Estabil raised his cup.

"Once there was a Rad of Takkor," he said, "who, wandering through his marshlands saw an Ulf maiden about to be done to death by a savage monster of the air. The Rad slew the monster and rescued the Ulf maiden, who proved to be the daughter of the Vil of the Ulfi. Every Ulf, from the Vil to his lowliest subject, will never forget. And in this cup we pledge to the Rad of Takkor our eternal friendship."

He and Eriné both raised their cups to their lips, and Thorne followed their example. "The Rad of Takkor gratefully accepts the pledge of friendship of the Ulfi," he said, "and is deeply sensible of the honor thus bestowed upon him. In return, he pledges his lasting friendship to Estabil, his lovely daughter, and his loyal subjects."

As soon as they had emptied their cups, Estabil raised his hand. Behind him the gong sounded twice, and a dozen Ulf warriors, flying six on a side, emerged from the mouth of a cave high on the hillside, bearing between them a rectangle of silken fabric about eight feet long and four wide. They alighted in front of the Vil, and saluted.

"The Rad of Takkor is ready to be conveyed to the house of Thaine," he said. Then he turned to Thorne. "Seat yourself in the middle of the cloth, my lord," he invited, "and you will be carried swiftly and safely to your destination."

Though he was not entirely reassured as to the safety of this fragile conveyance, Thorne did as directed.

The Vil raised his hand. The gong sounded three strokes. Then the wings of the twelve Ulf warriors began whirring rapidly, and Thorne felt himself rising. All around him the Ulfi burst into song. He waved farewell. A moment later he was gliding over the treetops, the Ulf-song swiftly dying in the distance.

Presently they flew out over a lake, in the center of which was an island. Straight to the island they took him, and set him down in the midst of it in a small clearing.

One of the Ulf warriors touched his arm and pointed. "There is the house of Thaine."

Thorne gazed intently in the direction the little fellow indicated. Presently he was able to make out what had entirely escaped his attention before—a small, irregularly shaped stone house, camouflaged with vines and creepers, and surrounded by trees.

"Ah, I see it now. I am beholden to you and your Vil for this favor. Please convey my thanks to him."

One of the little warriors rolled the cloth into a bundle and thrust it beneath his arm. All twelve of them saluted and swiftly faded from view.

He crossed the clearing, and entering an opening in the vines, found a large circular doorway cut in the stone. The door stood open, revealing a large room with several swinging chairs, suspended divans, and a fireplace. Three circular doorways cut in the walls led to other rooms.

"Thaine," he called, then waited expectantly.

There was no answer.

He was about to call her a second time when he suddenly heard a low growl from one of the rooms beyond. Then, out of that room streaked a huge black-haired beast with short legs, webbed feet, a paddle-shaped tail armed with spikes, and a cavernous mouth as large as that of a crocodile. He instantly recognized it as a dalf.

There was but one thing to do, and that quickly. Thorne seized the handle of the great door of thick planking, and swung it shut. A moment later he felt the impact of the heavy beast on the other side. He kept his hand on the latch, and it was well that he did so, for he suddenly felt that it was being pressed upward from the other side. Recalling the remarkable sagacity of these creatures, he was convinced that the beast was trying to open the door.

He was looking around for something with which to brace the latch, when he suddenly heard another growl, this time behind him. Turning, he beheld a second dalf, black with a ring of bright yellow fur circling its neck, swiftly bearing down upon him.

CHAPTER 18

When he saw the second dalf charging toward him, Thorne whipped out his sword and raised it to defend himself. But he lowered it again.

"Tezzu!" he exclaimed.

At this the demeanor of the beast suddenly changed. Instead of charging, it now bounded playfully up to him, then began skipping and leaping around him and making little purring noises deep in its throat.

And now, in the same leafy opening through which the beast had appeared, he saw a slender, girlish figure carrying a basket of fish and a trident.

"Thaine!" he cried.

"Hahr Ree Thorne! It's really you! I'm so glad!"

Dropping basket and trident, she ran forward, flung her arms around his neck and, much to his amazement, kissed him.

"I thought you would never come. I feared they had killed you."

"They tried hard enough," he replied, "but I got away and came as soon as I could."

"I'm sure you did. Let us go inside while I prepare something to eat. Why do you stand there holding the latch?"

"Because one of your dalfs is on the other side, trying to get at me."

"That's Neem. He won't molest you, now that I am here."

Thus reassured, Thorne opened the door. Neem, the great black dalf, waddled out to meet his mistress, but paid no attention to the Earthman. The latter picked up the basket and trident, and they went in.

Thorne insisted upon helping Thaine prepare the meal, and they soon had pulcho brewing, fish grilling, and fresh cakes baking.

"From your floral decorations, I judge that you have been among the Little People," said Thaine, as she turned a browned slab of fish.

"You judge correctly," Thorne replied. "In fact it was a dozen of their warriors who brought me here. Then they saluted and disappeared. Do you know anything about that strange power of theirs—making themselves invisible?"

"I've seen them do it many times," she told him, "yet how they do it remains a mystery. Our scientists believe they are able to surround themselves with auras of photo-electric force which cause light rays to bend around them and anything within the auras, such as their weapons and clothing. Since we see objects only by means of light rays reflected from them into our eyes, if the rays miss them or bend around them they are invisible to us."

"Sounds reasonable enough," said Thorne. "But what is this force?"

"One might as well ask, 'What is electricity, or magnetism, or gravity?' We know that when they are very weary, or weakened by wounds or illness, they are unable to generate this strange force."

"That explains why Eriné was visible when pursued by the bat. She must have been exhausted."

"The bat?"

Thorne told her how he had saved the life of the daughter of the Vil of the Ulfi, and showed her the ring.

"It is a precious gift, and one not lightly bestowed," said Thaine. "I have one like it, and so has my father, but only because he once saved the life of the Vil of the Little People."

"You remind me, that we were to go in search of your father. Have you had any word from him?"

"None. Even the Ulfi are baffled, and they know almost everything that takes place in this marsh. I fear I shall never see him again."

Thorne saw the tears gathering in her eyes. "We'll find your father, never fear," he said reassuringly. "And now that the food is ready, let us eat, and I will tell you of my adventures since I last saw you. I owe you an explanation for staying away so long."

When he had finished, she pounced on that very part of the story which he most wished to forget. "This Neva, is she very beautiful?"

"Very, even though she is deceitful and cruel."

"You love her?"

"Would you love a person who had tricked you—then condemned you to a horrible, lingering death?"

"That," said Thaine, refilling his pulcho cup for him, "is not an answer but an evasion."

"Well then, if you must have it, I wish I had never seen her. But I bore you with these troubles of mine. Let us speak no more of them."

"My poor Hahr Ree Thorne," she said. "You do not bore me. Your troubles are my troubles, for are we not true friends?"

"Thaine," he said, "you *are* a real friend."

"I am glad," she said softly, and laid her cheek against his shoulder.

Presently she leaned forward, half turned, and gazed up into his face. "Look at me, Hahr Ree Thorne. Is this Neva really so much more beautiful than I?"

"What a question!" he exclaimed. "It's just like a woman to think of a poser like that."

"Another evasion," she countered, "but it tells me what I wanted to find out. She *is* more beautiful."

He studied her smilingly. "I wouldn't say so. She is a blonde, you are a brunette. She is a great beauty of her type, and you of yours. You and Neva are gems of equal luster, but different."

"Why, then, perhaps I can make you forget this Neva."

Before he was aware of what she was about, she had turned still more—was lying back across his arm. Her eyes were dark wells of enchantment. Her red lips, half parted, drew him seductively.

"Why don't you kiss me?" she pouted.

"You little witch!"

Fiercely he bent down—crushed those warm red lips against his own.

For a moment, she suffered his caress, unresisting. Then, with a little frightened gasp she broke from his embrace—returned to her place beside the pulcho jar. Mechanically, she filled their cups. Tears trembled on her long, dark lashes. Her lips quivered ever so slightly as she handed him his cup.

"Why, Thaine, what's wrong?" he asked.

"I—I didn't know it would be like that," she quavered.

"You don't really love me, then?"

"I wish I really knew."

At this juncture there was the noise of huge wings flapping overhead, followed by a thud. Thorne knew from the sounds that a gawr had just flown over the house and landed in the clearing. Both dalfs sprang up, growling ominously, but Thaine silenced them.

Then, accompanied by Thorne, she ran to the door and peered through the leafy screen.

CHAPTER 19

When Thorne looked out through the leafy screen that camouflaged the door of Thaine's island home, he saw that a warrior in the uniform of an officer of the Kamud had dismounted in the clearing. The fellow was leading his gawr beneath the branches of a large, spreading tree, where the bird-beast would be concealed from observers flying overhead. The newcomer walked with the peculiar, rolling gait of a man whose legs are abnormally short in proportion to the rest of his body.

"It's Yirl Du!" Thorne exclaimed.

Keeping cautiously beneath the trees which fringed the clearing, Yirl Du circled toward the house. A few moments later he entered the opening in the screen. To Thorne he rendered the usual salutation, but to Thaine, the royal salute. This surprised the Earthman until he remembered that she was the daughter of Miradon Vil, and therefore entitled to the homage due a princess.

"I have news—momentous news," said Yirl Du as he entered the hut.

"Have—have you news of my father?" Thaine asked, anxiously.

"Ill news," he replied. "His majesty is in the clutches of Sel Han, who has imprisoned him in Castle Takkor."

"We must find a way to rescue him," exclaimed Thorne.

"Wait, I have not told you all," Yirl Du said. "Perhaps I had best begin at the beginning. After I was netted by Sel Han's Ma Gongi, they searched a while for you, my lord. But at last they gave up the chase and flew with me to Castle Takkor. I found the castle garrisoned entirely by Ma Gongi, with Sur Det and a few of his cronies in command. Sur Det had been rescued from the prison pen by Sel Han.

"It seems that some time ago the yellow scientists rediscovered how to generate the deadly green ray used in warfare by their ancestors. Since then they have been building large ray projectors, not as yet being able to manufacture small hand projectors powerful enough for efficient use. With four of these projectors and an army of Ma Gongi mounted on gawrs, Sel Han yesterday flew to Dukor, overawed the army and the people with the weapons he had brought with him, and took over the government. He captured all the high officers of the Kamud, and it is said he intends to proclaim himself Vil of Xancibar in a day or two. These officers, among whom are Kov Lutas and Lal Vak, together with the Dixtar and his daughter Neva, were sent to Castle Takkor, where they are now prisoners, guarded by the Ma Gongi warriors.

"Miradon Vil, who had previously been captured by Sel Han's Ma Gongi scouts, was at first held in the secret camp where they were making the ray projectors. But as soon as the government had been over-thrown, Sel Han ordered him brought to Castle Takkor, where he could be guarded with the other important prisoners.

"Sur Det ordered me imprisoned in a room in one of the towers, to await the arrival of Sel Han, who would then decide what my fate should be. But, unfortunately for his plans, he had me put in a room in which there was a hidden panel which communicated with a secret passageway that led to the underground cellars, and thence out under the docks.

"I lost no time in making use of this means of escape, but ran into one of Sel Han's officers. I caught him by the throat before he could make a sound, and hung on until he ceased to breathe. Then I donned his uniform and weapons, and boldly ascended to the dock. There, by virtue of the authority vested in my borrowed uniform, I demanded and received a gawr from one of the attendants, and flew away unmolested."

"Do you think it would be possible for you and me to return to the castle, enter by way of the secret passage, and rescue Miradon Vil?" Thorne asked.

"I fear it would not, my lord," Yirl Du answered. "His majesty is too well guarded. He is an even more important prisoner than Irintz Tel. Sel Han holds him as a hostage to prevent any uprising among the royalists, just as he holds the Dixtar to keep the loyal Kamudists from revolting."

"How many ray projectors are left at the castle?" Thorne asked.

"There are none," Yirl Du told him. "All four are in use in Dukor. Where Sel Han goes, there go the projectors, also. He will not leave them in the hands of his most trusted officers, for they are his very lifeblood. Without them he could be easily defeated by a handful of regular soldiers. And so far as I know, no others have been completed."

"Why, then, perhaps we can take the castle," mused Thorne. "You told me once that the Free Swordsmen would revolt against the rule of any but a rad of the Takkor blood."

"I'm sure they are loyal, my lord," Yirl Du said. "You have but to command, and they will fight to the last man to recover your castle for you."

"Good. I think it can be done without heavy losses. I have a plan."

That afternoon, shortly after Thorne had outlined his plan and given his instructions to Yirl Du, the latter flew away in the direction of Takkor City.

Some time later, when the shadows had begun to lengthen, Thorne, who had been snatching forty winks on one of Thaine's divans, was awakened by her hand on his brow.

"The time has come," she said.

Thorne sat up, drank the cup of freshly brewed pulcho she proffered him, and sprang to the floor.

"Now if you will be so kind as to lend me Tezzu and a boat," he said, "I'll be off."

"Why do you say 'lend,'" she asked, "when I am going with you?"

"You are to remain here. There will be fighting—bloodshed. It is too dangerous."

She drew herself up proudly. "I am a warrior, and as good a swordsman as the man you just sent to rally your followers. If you won't take me with you I shall go in a separate boat."

Seeing the impossibility of dissuading her from her resolve, Thorne set about making preparations for their journey. They then took Tezzu with them, leaving Neem, the other beast, to guard the house, and went down to the boat.

Tezzu, with the tow-rope in his huge mouth, swiftly took them across the lake and into a narrow stream where the foliage arching overhead concealed them from the sight of flying enemies. After traversing a veritable network of these tiny streams and crossing a number of small lakes, they reached the shore of Takkor Lake just before sundown.

At the command of his mistress, Tezzu dragged the boat up out of the water, upon which ice crystals were already beginning to form, and into a place of concealment, where he was left to guard it. Then the man and girl set off along the lake shore, following the same route that Thorne had followed upon his first disastrous visit to Castle Takkor, and carefully keeping out of sight among the trees.

They had not traveled far before the sun set, so they were forced to pick their way through the undergrowth by the light of the nearer moon. Shortly thereafter, Yirl Du appeared in the path before them.

"Everything is arranged," he said softly. "I have been waiting to lead you to the rendezvous."

They paused only long enough to draw up their boots and let down their head-cloaks for warmth. Then Yirl Du led them away through the glittering, frost-coated jungle. Presently they came to a large clearing where several hundred warriors, mounted on gawrs, were assembled, and more were arriving constantly from all points of the compass, singly and in small groups. There was also a group of fifty warriors who were unmounted.

"In a little while there will be five hundred mounted warriors here, my lord," said Yirl Du. "My son, Rid Du, has assembled a thousand more afoot. They are scattered about in the city, seemingly only amusing themselves, but will rally to him at the signal, half to capture the gawrs on the wharf and the other half to rush the castle gate."

Shortly thereafter the last flying warrior arrived.

After a brief final conference with Thorne, Yirl Du led his foot-soldiers away. They were picked men, for they were to follow Yirl Du through the secret passageway into the castle and then capture and throw open the gates, so the soldiers under Rid Du could rush in.

Thorne was to lead the air attack which was calculated first to draw the attention of the defenders from Yirl Du's little party, and later to assist in crushing the Ma Gongi guards.

After he had waited for the length of time agreed upon with Yirl Du, Thorne gave the signal to his men, and one by one the great bird-beasts left the ground. With the Earthman in the lead, they formed a long line which ascended for about two thousand feet, then straightened out to fly directly for the castle. Once above his objective, Thorne led the way downward in a swift, descending spiral which, as it neared the upper parapets, flattened into a great circle that followed the outline of the walls.

An alarm had been sounded at the first approach of this flying host, and now, as they drew nearer, javelins flew up at them, hurled by the defenders on the walls. Assisted by the force of gravity, while their enemies were impeded by it, the flying warriors were able to reply to good purpose, and soon there were many dead and wounded Ma Gongi on the ramparts. But it seemed that as fast as they fell more rushed up to take their places.

At the first alarm, five hundred of Rid Du's warriors had swarmed down over the docks where the gawrs were kept. As they were guarded only by a few soldiers and orderlies, the bird-beasts were soon captured. In the meantime, led by Rid Du, the other half of his little company assembled before the gate and began hurtling javelins up at the defenders.

Now was the time for Yirl Du to strike, and Thorne watched tensely. Presently he saw the little company emerge from one of the castle doors, quickly form a flying wedge with Yirl Du at the apex, and charge across the courtyard, cutting down or scattering the surprised Ma Gongi in their way. Just before the gate the two wings of the wedge divided, and each column ascended into one of the watch towers which guarded the gateway. A moment later the gates swung open, and in poured the Free Swordsmen from the town, with Rid Du at their head.

Now Thorne's flying warriors swooped down into the melee, abandoning their javelins for fear of injuring their comrades, and fighting at close range with sword, mace and dagger. The slaughter was appalling. The Ma Gongi, most of whom had been slaves and were unaccustomed to warfare, were no match for the disciplined Takkor swordsmen.

The ramparts and courtyard were thickly strewn with their bodies as Thorne, with Yirl Du, Thaine, and a small contingent of Takkor swordsmen, cut down the warriors who guarded the entrance, charged into the castle, and began their search for the prisoners.

Yirl Du led the way to the great central tower, then fought their way up the winding staircase, the yellow defenders stubbornly contesting each step of the way.

Thorne and Yirl Du were ever in the front as they climbed the stairs, and both were soon covered with wounds. When they reached the flight which led to the top story, they met with the most desperate resistance they had yet encountered. But the swiftly flashing blade of the Earthman backed up the swords of Yirl Du and Thaine, and the javelins of the warriors who came behind them soon cleared the stairs of living enemies, and the few who remained above to contest their way were quickly cut down.

Thorne tried the door and found it barred on the inside. Reversing his bloody sword, he beat upon the panels with the pommel.

"Who is it?" came a cautious call from within.

"The Rad of Takkor," Thorne replied. "Open quickly."

At this, there was the sound of a sliding bolt, and the door swung open. A tall, broad-shouldered man whose shaggy hair and flowing beard gleamed golden yellow under the baridium lights stood in the doorway.

At sight of him, Yirl Du and the other warriors instantly raised both hands before their eyes and muttered the royal salutation, while Thaine, with an exclamation of joy, ran forward and flung her arms around his neck.

"Father!" she cried. "I'm so glad we found you safe."

Gently he took her face between his huge hands, and bending, kissed her forehead. "Little daughter!" he murmured. "This was man's work. You should not have come."

"Did you not train me to do a man's work? And have I not done it well? Ask Sheb Takkor."

Thorne, who had instantly sensed that this regal looking personage must be Miradon Vil, had only been a shade behind the others in rendering the royal salutation. He now stood, respectfully waiting for the Vil to speak.

"It is a question I need not propound," said Miradon. "I know you have fought nobly, or you would not be here. But, come, Sheb Takkor Rad, and you, Yirl Du Jen. There are those in other apartments who will be glad to thank their gallant rescuers."

He led the way down the hall and tapped on a door. From within came a little squeaky voice, which Thorne immediately recognized as that of Irintz Tel. "Who is there?"

"Miradon Vil with friends who have rescued us. Open."

The bolt slid back, the door swung open, and the little rat-faced Dixtar stepped out, followed by Kov Lutas and Lal Vak.

"Where's Neva?" squeaked Irintz Tel. "Have you found my daughter?"

"She should be in one of these apartments," replied Miradon Vil.

"Open the doors! Break them down!" ordered the Dixtar, with a wave of his hand. "Why do you all stand there, staring?"

Thorne regarded him coldly. "You forget, Irintz Tel," he said, "that this is my castle and these are my warriors. They take orders only from me."

At this, the Dixtar turned deathly pale, but Thorne, ignoring him, warmly greeted the handsome young Kov Lutas and the white-haired Lal Vak, both of whom profusely thanked him for coming to their rescue.

In the meantime, Miradon Vil had gone on to the next door and rapped. Thorne's heart gave a great bound as he heard the voice that answered—the voice of Neva.

Irintz Tel rushed to the door and embraced his daughter as she stepped out, followed by two of her slave-girls. Kov Lutas and Lal Vak instantly crowded forward to greet her, and the latter ceremoniously introduced Miradon Vil.

Thorne held aloof, watching them, his breast seething with conflicting emotions. Despite his resolve to put Neva forever from his thoughts, he now found that sight of her had suddenly reawakened all the old longing with redoubled intensity.

Suddenly he realized that Neva had seen him—was coming toward him—holding out her arms to him. His heart throbbed wildly. Yet he resolutely steeled himself to break the subtle spell she had again cast over him—forcing his flagging will to recall her betrayal of him and the hideous death to which she had condemned him.

"Sheb, beloved!" she murmured. "The time has been so long . . ."

"The Dixtar's daughter," he said with frigid politeness, "honors the lowly castle of the Rad of Takkor by her charming presence. The Takkor retainers will have instructions to do all in their power to make her stay a pleasant one."

With this he saluted stiffly, and walked to where Yirl Du stood awaiting his orders. "See that these, my honored guests, are given the best the castle affords."

"Yes, my lord."

For a moment Neva stood bewildered. Then a sudden flush suffused her lovely face. Turning, she reentered her apartment, head held high and eyes flashing.

Without even glancing at the door through which she had vanished, Thorne addressed Yirl Du. "I understand that the chief officials of the Kamud, including the seven judges, are confined here."

"They are in the west wing, my lord."

"Have them brought here, Jen," cut in Irintz Tel imperiously. "We would speak with them."

"They are to be kept in their quarters, and well guarded," continued Thorne. "Also, you are to search for Sur Det, and if he still lives, bring him to me. I would question him."

"Yes, my lord."

The Earthman now turned to the little Dixtar. "I trust it will not be necessary to again remind you that my warriors take orders only from me."

Irintz Tel shot him a venomous glance. Then he swung on his heel and entered Neva's apartment.

Thorne looked at Miradon Vil with an apologetic smile. "I hope that your majesty will excuse me, as I have pressing duties. Preparations must be made at once, so we can all leave the castle before morning. Sel Han may return at any moment with his ray projectors, and if he finds us here our case will be desperate, if not entirely hopeless."

The Vil returned his smile. "I understand. Can I help?"

"No, I thank your majesty."

Thorne hurried down the corpse-littered stairs, and out into the courtyard. Here he set about making immediate preparations for flight, ordering that all available weapons and provisions be brought out and loaded onto the gawrs. He planned to leave the Vil and Thaine in their secret hiding place, and to find another for Irintz Tel and Neva. Then he would lead his warriors far out into the marsh and hide from Sel Han and his fearsome new weapons until he could devise some plan for successfully combating him.

He was overseeing these preparations some time later, when Yirl Du came and asked to speak with him aside.

"My lord," he said, "Sur Det cannot be found among either the dead or the living."

"Then he has escaped. We must hasten our preparations, for he has undoubtedly gone to Dukor, and will bring Sel Han and his ray projectors down upon us."

But the words had scarcely left his mouth when a guard called from one of the towers: "A vast host of warriors mounted on gawrs is approaching. Also there are a score of the great metal gawrs."

Instantly, confusion reigned in the castle. A frightened warrior leaped on the back of a half-loaded gawr and jerked the guiding rod. The bird-beast flapped awkwardly up out of the courtyard. But it had scarcely cleared the castle walls when a strange and terrible thing happened. A green ray shot out from somewhere beyond the wall—struck the fleeing warrior and his mount. For an instant they were visible, bathed in that weird, green light. Then they seemed to suddenly shrivel and disintegrate. Where they had been there was nothing at all. The ray winked out and consternation settled over the courtyard.

CHAPTER 20

Thorne knew that Sel Han, with his powerful ray projectors, could not only cut off any attempt at flight, but could destroy the castle and all in it at his pleasure. Yet he resolved that he, his friends and his followers should not succumb without resisting to the utmost. He accordingly rallied his panic-stricken warriors to the defense of the walls, then mounted to the ramparts to survey the movements of the enemy.

Sel Han, it seemed, was not disposed immediately to storm the castle. All of his flying machines had alighted well out of javelin range of the walls, and from the interiors of these, Ma Gongi foot-soldiers were pouring. A ray projector had been mounted on the flat roof of a nearby house, and Thorne stared at it curiously. It looked much like a large telescope on a conical stand. The flying warriors were circling the castle, but the great bulk of these were alighting on the ground. Soon only a few remained in the air as scouts and observers.

Glancing out over the lake, the Earthman saw that a second projector was mounted there on a large boat. He walked around the walls and descried a third on the roof of a building to the landward side, and still farther, a fourth, mounted on the ground to command the remaining sector of the wall.

Having completed his inspection of the disposal of the enemy troops and projectors, Thorne returned to a parapet beside the gate which opened on the dock, and before which Sel Han had massed his chief officers.

As he stood there on the battlement, watching every movement of the enemy, he heard a group of people coming up behind him. Turning, he beheld Miradon Vil and Irintz Tel walking side by side. Though they had always been deadly enemies it was evident that they had united to make common cause against the man who not only threatened them, but all of Mars as well.

Behind the two ex-rulers of Xancibar came Neva escorted by Lal Vak, and Thaine escorted by Kov Lutas. All carried weapons.

"We sought you out, Sheb Takkor Rad, hoping that we might be of some assistance in the defense," said Miradon Vil.

"I fear there is little we can do save surrender or die, your majesty, though I have resolved that I, personally, will fight to the death rather than surrender to Sel Han."

"Your resolve coincides with my own," replied Miradon Vil.

"And mine! And mine!" chorused the others, with the single exception of Irintz Tel.

The ominous silence that followed was suddenly rent by the clarion notes of a trumpet. Hurrying to the wall, Thorne saw that a man had detached himself from the group around Sel Han, and walked to a point before the gate just out of range of a hurled javelin.

Once again the herald sounded a ringing call on his trumpet. Then, resting his instrument on his hip, he cried: "His Imperial Majesty, Sel Han the Invincible, Vil of Xancibar, Vil of Vils, and Vildus of all Mars, commands that Sheb Takkor and his warriors instantly lay down their weapons and come forth from the castle gates unarmed. His majesty has it in his power to utterly destroy the castle and every soul within it. Witness!"

He paused dramatically, and as he paused a pencil of green light stabbed out from the projector on the house-top. It flashed to the top of one of the lesser towers, and where the ray touched, the crystal blocks and mortar shriveled and vanished, leaving a jagged hole in the battlement.

The ray winked out, and the herald continued: "There will be no terms of surrender, other than such conditions as the Vildus of Mars shall see fit to impose."

With a farewell flourish of his trumpet, he turned and walked back to where Sel Han and his officers stood waiting.

Thorne turned to an officer who stood near by. "Get me a herald."

The officer ran to the gate tower and immediately emerged with a youth who carried a trumpet. Thorne gave him his instructions, and mounting the wall, he blew a ringing flourish. After waiting for a moment, he announced: "The Lord of Takkor, his warriors and his friends, defy Sel Han of the empty titles, and his bandits, who have invaded the Takkor domain. Here is Castle Takkor, and here are its defenders unafraid, for Sel Han to come and take if he can, or to destroy if he has aught to gain by wanton destruction. The Lord of Takkor further states . . ."

The speech of the herald was suddenly cut off, along with his life, by a green flash from the ray projector on the house-top.

A roar of rage went up from the Takkor swordsmen. If Sel Han had thought to frighten them by this demonstration he had a poor conception of the caliber of these men.

But though this had made the Takkor warriors more steadfast in their purpose, there was at least one occupant of the castle upon whom it had worked the opposite effect. Chancing to look toward Irintz Tel, Thorne noticed that he was trembling violently.

Presently there came two more blasts from the trumpet of Sel Han's herald.

"His Imperial Majesty, the Vildus of Mars, could destroy the castle and all it contains," shouted the herald, "yet he is just and merciful. He realizes that the warriors of the Takkor Rad and the prisoners are respectively under the command—and in the power of a man who is willing to sacrifice them all to satisfy his own empty vanity and make good his puny defiance of Sel Han, the Invincible.

"Wherefore, his imperial majesty gives you, each and every one, a respite from death, during which you may have time to depose this foolhardy leader and save your own lives. And to the man who will bring him the head of Sheb Takkor, the Vildus of Mars covenants to present the Raddek of Takkor with all its lands. His majesty decrees that your respite from death shall last from now until the planet has completed one turn upon its axis. If, by that time and at that very moment, you have not obeyed his edict, then will the castle and all in it be utterly destroyed."

Having said his say, the herald returned to the group of officers.

"Looks as if things have quieted down for the present, at least," said Thorne, turning to the others. "I suggest that we all get some much needed sleep."

"One moment, Sheb Takkor," interposed Irintz Tel. "I suggest that before we retire we hold a council and decide just what we are going to do. It is only fair that we should all have some say in the matter."

"I quite agree to that," Thorne replied. "Thus far I have been acting under the belief that I was carrying out the wishes of the majority in defying Sel Han. If I have erred, there is yet time to rectify the mistake. Let us go into the castle."

They gathered, a few moments later, in the apartment which Thorne had chosen for himself. The Earthman had asked Yirl Du to attend as the representative of the Free Swordsmen. The others were Neva, Thaine, Miradon Vil, Irintz Tel, Lal Vak, and Kov Lutas.

Thorne stood at a taboret in the center of the room, filling cups with steaming pulcho, a jar of which had just been brought in by Yirl Du. These he passed to his assembled guests. Then he said to Irintz Tel, "Since it was at your suggestion that this council was assembled, I will call upon you first to address us."

The Dixtar took a dainty sip of pulcho, then carefully held the cup before him.

"My good friends and comrades in adversity," he began, "I, for one, see the hopelessness of our position here, and the futility of further resistance to the decree of fate. After all, it is better to be live prisoners than dead heroes, blasted into nothingness by the awful weapons of the Ma Gongi. I suggest that we surrender to Sel Han while he is inclined to be merciful, thus not only saving our own lives, but those of the brave Takkor swordsmen who sought to rescue us from the conqueror."

"You have all heard the suggestion of the Dixtar," said Thorne. "Will you surrender or resist?"

"Resist!" they cried unanimously.

Then the Dixtar, who for ten long Martian years had never been gainsaid in anything, went suddenly pale. "I fear," he said, "that you will all regret this rash decision when regret comes too late." Then he turned, clasped his hands behind his back, and with his chin sunk on his chest, strode out of the room. The others soon followed to go to their several apartments.

The Earthman, left alone, prepared to retire. One thing kept recurring to him as he hooded the baridium globes and crept into bed. It was the fact that as Kov Lutas walked out between the two girls, he had seemed more attentive to Thaine than to Neva. Yirl Du had told Thorne that the young officer avowed undying love for the beautiful daughter of the Dixtar. Thorne was puzzled.

He soon fell asleep, but it seemed to him that he had not slumbered for more than a few moments when he was awakened by a sharp tug at his coverlets. He looked up sleepily.

"Yirl Du!" he exclaimed. "What's wrong?"

"I have made a startling discovery, my lord," Yirl Du replied, "else I should not have disturbed your rest."

"I'm sure of that," said Thorne. "What is it?"

For answer, his henchman drew a scroll from beneath his cloak. After passing it to the Earthman, he walked to the lever and unhooded the baridium globes, flooding the room with light.

CHAPTER 21

Thorne glanced curiously over the scroll given him by Yirl Du. Then he threw back the covers and leaped out of bed.

"Where did you get this?" he demanded. "Where is Irintz Tel?"

"The traitor is in his own bed, and probably asleep by now," replied Yirl Du.

"But what of Sel Han? Did Irintz Tel get a message through to him, and was there a reply?"

"He did, and I have the reply also." Yirl Du plucked a second scroll from beneath his cloak and handed it to Thorne, who perused it carefully, then re-read the other message.

The correspondence went in this order, the first letter full of hasty revisions:

> TO SEL HAN, VILDUS OF MARS,
> Salutation and submission:
> With my help you can take Castle Takkor and all in it, sustaining but trifling losses. Tomorrow night, in the period of darkness between the setting of the nearer moon and the rising of the farther, quietly mass a thousand men near the lake gate. Have another group of fifty warriors bring a long stout rope, knotted for easy climbing, beneath the point where I stand when I hurl this note. I will drop a cord to draw up and make fast the rope for them. Then we will cut down the guards and throw open the gates. With a thousand of your foot-soldiers in the courtyard and your mounted warriors attacking from above, there can be but one outcome. I seek to make no terms, but align myself wholeheartedly with your cause, and now await your reply and your commands.
>
> IRINTZ TEL

> TO IRINTZ TEL,

Salutation and greetings:

Your plan pleases me. As soon as the sky grows dark, lower your cord with a muffled weight at the end. When you feel two tugs on the cord draw up the rope which we shall tie on the other end, and lash it to a merlon. As soon as it is secure, tug twice, and we will do the rest.

If, through your efforts, we are able to capture the castle, I will make you Vil of Xancibar or any other vilet of equal size which you may choose, and Neva shall share with me the throne of all Mars.

SEL HAN VILDUS OF MARS.

"Ah! So that's their game. They will capture the towers, throw open the gates, and take us by surprise during the dark interval."

"They will unless we prevent Irintz Tel from drawing up their rope for them. Shall I place him under arrest?"

"No. Let him sleep. There is nothing he can do before tomorrow night, and I already have the glimmerings of a counter plan. In the meantime, tell me how you got these documents."

"It was quite simple, my lord. As you know, I am familiar with every secret passageway in this castle. When Irintz Tel left the conference I suspected him of some treachery, so I followed. Seeing him enter his apartment, I slipped into a hidden passageway which leads to a panel in the central room of his suite. There, through a small peep-hole, I spied upon him. He seemed quite agitated, and finally went to the writing board and composed this letter. He made a copy, probably because, as you see, the original is full of corrections and crossed-out words.

"Next, he unraveled the silken lining of one of his garments and wound the long cord he obtained therefrom into a ball. He thrust the ball of cord and the copy of the corrected scroll under his cloak, and went out. On the way out he hurled this original letter into the fireplace. Luckily I was able to open the panel, run to the fireplace, and rescue it before it caught fire.

"I read the note, and followed Irintz Tel. I saw him tie the cylinder to the end of his silken cord and hurl it out toward the enemy camp where it was picked up by a yellow warrior. Some time later Sel Han's reply came, and Irintz Tel drew it up on the wall.

"With a false beard and tattered cloak, I disguised myself as a castle menial. Again I spied upon Irintz Tel in his room. Presently I saw him place Sel Han's answer on the writing board, and resolved to attempt to get it without arousing his suspicion. Accordingly, I went into his room with a load of wood, managed to upset the writing board, shake the scroll out of the cylinder, thrust it into my belt, and hand him the empty cylinder, which he immediately tossed into the fire."

"Obviously Irintz Tel thinks both of these documents were burned, and so imagines himself safe from discovery. That fits in splendidly with my plan."

"But aren't you going to arrest him and punish him?"

"No. I have a more subtle scheme than that. Say nothing about these notes or the Dixtar's treachery to anyone. Leave all to me. Tomorrow, go about your duties as if nothing is amiss. And now get yourself some rest. I'm going back to bed."

Thorne was up with the sun, and instantly set about his task. First he put his men to work cleaning up the place and tending the gawrs. Then, accompanied by Yirl Du, he explored the underground chambers of the castle. It was not long before he had mapped out a route leading through the largest doorways and archways to a point near one of the concealed entrances of the secret passageway, through which Yirl Du had previously escaped, and which led underneath the docks. After investigating this passageway and the space beneath the docks, he returned to the castle cellar.

"Bring me six skilled masons," he told Yirl Du, "and have them conceal their tools on the way so there will be no suspicion of what we are about to do. I'll wait here."

Yirl Du hurried away, and presently returned with six members of the Free Swordsmen, carrying tools and mortar concealed in two large food hampers.

Thorne addressed them. "I want you to remove the blocks from the wall at this point, until you have made an opening large enough for a gawr to pass through. Then wait here with your tools for further orders, which will not come until tonight. Food and pulcho will be sent you."

Accompanied by Yirl Du, he crossed the room and stepped through the large doorway, carefully closing the door after him.

"Keep this door closed with two guards before it," he said, "and give them orders to admit nobody but you or me. You, yourself, will take food to the workmen at meal-times."

After the two guards had been posted, Thorne and Yirl Du paid a visit to the tower where the officers of the Kamud were imprisoned. These, the Earthman ordered transferred to a dungeon in the cellar. When this had been accomplished he returned to the battlements to direct the work there, and to keep watch over the enemy.

That afternoon, after Irintz Tel had retired to his apartment, Thorne issued secret instructions to his various officers. These, in turn, transmitted instructions to the men in their charge.

Miradon Vil, Kov Lutas, Lal Vak and the two girls were told nothing. Thorne did not want the Dixtar's daughter to know of the perfidy of her father until his own plans had been carried out.

Night came at last, with the transient brightness of the nearer moon. It was at the setting of this orb that all of Thorne's forces were to go into action. In the meantime, a secret watch was kept on Irintz Tel.

Presently Thorne, standing in the shadow, saw the Dixtar cross the courtyard, walking unconcernedly and saluting the officers and men he encountered. Leisurely he mounted to the wall and a moment later disappeared in the shadow of the tower.

Thorne softly called to Rid Du, who stood waiting. "Start out with the gawrs, and warn the men to be careful about making any unusual noise."

Led by a man who had been coached for the purpose until he thoroughly knew the route through the castle and cellar which had been mapped out by Thorne, the great bird-beasts, each carrying a rider, began forming in line and marching into the castle.

By the time the moon had set nearly two-thirds of the gawrs had entered the castle. At this moment all the warriors on the walls and in the towers began silently stealing from their posts, with the exception of the few who guarded the towers that controlled the lake gates. These had instructions to remain until the first attackers appeared, then flee down the inner stairways which led to the cellars, and join the others.

Thorne kept his post at the doorway until the last huge bird-beast had lumbered through. Then he closed and bolted the door on the inside, and ran up the steps of the central tower where, one by one, he aroused Neva, Thaine, Miradon Vil, Lal Vak and Kov Lutas.

"Come with me quickly, and make no sound," he told them. "The enemy is about to attack, and I have a plan to frustrate them. But we must be quiet."

They followed him down the stairway unquestioningly, Neva escorted by Miradon Vil, who seemed strangely solicitous of her safety; Thaine, attended by Kov Lutas, and Lal Vak walked with the Earthman. Thorne closed and bolted every door after them as they followed the route where the gawrs had walked through the castle and descended to the basement. Here, after passing through several rooms, and bolting each door behind them, they caught up with the end of a line of warriors, among whom Thorne recognized the guards from the gate towers. This line was swiftly and silently filing through the hole opened in the wall by the masons, who, since all the gawrs had passed, had begun to fill it up under the direction of Yirl Du.

Thorne bolted the last door and told his companions to follow the warriors through the opening. Then he approached Yirl Du. "Have you shown these men the secret passageway?"

"Yes, my lord. And I have instructed them to completely wall up the hole as soon as the last warrior has passed through, then follow by way of the passage."

"Good. Come with me, for we still have the most difficult part of our task to perform."

They hurried out to where the men and bird-beasts stood under the dock, amid the supporting pilings, and now heard the flapping of many wings above and around them.

"Sel Han's flying warriors are attacking the castle. Now is our chance, but we must work swiftly."

In accordance with his previous orders, a hundred of Thorne's warriors had divided themselves into four groups of twenty-five men, each under the command of an officer. The members of one of these groups, all young fellows under the command of Rid Du, had stripped themselves to their loin-cloths and were plastering each other from head to foot with a thick coating of heavy grease, working in the dim light of a small baridium torch held by another warrior. Stacked near them was a pile of large crocks made from transparent material.

As soon as they were thoroughly greased, each man belted sword, mace and dagger about him, then took up a crock, inverted it, and lifted it over his head, so it rested upon his shoulders. They marched down to the water's edge, and Rid Du, who was in the lead, chopped a hole in the thin ice with his mace, then stepped into it and disappeared from view, still holding the crock over his head. His companions followed him, one by one, until all had dropped out of sight.

"Do you think they'll make it?" Thorne asked anxiously. "Looks as if they might run out of air before they reach the boat."

"Don't worry, my lord," Yirl Du replied. "All are trained divers. Every one of them could walk out to the boat and back again without danger of suffocating. And when they break through the ice around that boat the crew of the ray projector will have short shrift, with the exception of the operator whom you ordered kept alive."

"I hope you are right," said Thorne, "and you should know if any one does. Now, it is time for us to attack the other projector crews. I'll take the one on the west, you the one on the north, and Ven Hitus the one to the east. Come!"

He leaped into the saddle of a gawr held ready for him, and swiftly led the way to the west end of the dock, the great bird-beasts of his twenty-five warriors lumbering after him on the frozen ground. At the end of the dock a large ramp led up under a warehouse, open toward the lake after the manner of a lean-to. He rode out through the front of this and reconnoitered for a moment. By now there was a tremendous commotion in the castle. Baridium torches were flashing all about, and by their light he could see the warriors milling on the walls, while others mounted on gawrs circled the towers and battlements.

But what chiefly concerned him now was the ray projector which he was to capture, and which Sel Han had mounted on a house-top. He marked its position by the faint glow of the light on its instrument board. Then, with a whispered "Now!" to his fighting men, who had assembled around him, he pulled up on the guiding rod, and his bird-beast launched itself into the air.

In a few moments they were soaring above their objective, which was only about five hundred yards from the dock. Then they dived downward in a steep spiral.

The crew of the ray projector had paid no attention to the sound of gawrs flapping above their heads, evidently taking these to be the mounts of their own warriors. And so, when the great bird-beasts alighted on the roof around them, and Thorne's fighting men sprang upon them with drawn swords, they were taken completely by surprise.

Thorne made straight for the operator, who leaped up to meet him; the Earthman's blade quickly sent his weapon spinning, and he clapped his hands over his eyes in token of surrender. The Takkor swordsmen made short work of the others.

Setting two men to guard his prisoner, Thorne raised his baridium torch above his head and unhooded it three times in succession. A moment later he saw it answered by three flashes from the projector on the north, and knew that Yirl Du had succeeded in capturing it. Then came a signal from the one on the east, announcing the success of Ven Hitus, and shortly thereafter another from the projector on the boat, now under the control of Rid Du.

Thorne called a warrior to his side.

"Fly back to the dock," he ordered, "and tell them they can all come out now. Send fifty men to capture the airships, but let them go on foot. I want no one in the air except the man who is to carry dry clothing to Rid Du and his warriors on the boat. And let him return as soon as possible."

Thorne turned his attention to the instrument board of the ray projector. Though it held a half dozen dials with numbers and pointers on them, evidently to tell the operator how much of this or that charge or substance the mechanism contained, he was at present concerned only with the parts intended for manipulation by the operator.

These consisted of two small cranks and a lever. One crank, he soon found by testing it, elevated or lowered the muzzle of the projector, and the other turned it to the right or left. He pointed the muzzle upward where it could do no damage, and pulled the lever. A green flash shot skyward. He swiftly shut it off, and having mastered the weapon without the operator's assistance, ordered him bound.

A moment later the farther moon rose, flooding the scene with its pale light. After making sure that his men were in charge of Sel Han's airships, and that his warrior had returned from the boat, Thorne turned his attention to the castle.

Evidently Sel Han was still unaware that his projectors had been captured. Fully a thousand of his riders still circled above the walls on their bird-beasts. Thorne aimed the projector into the thick of these and pulled the lever. Instantly the green ray flashed out, cutting a great gap in the circle of flyers. And now from the north, south and east, the other projectors went into action.

The panic stricken riders who remained quickly dived for the nearest shelter—the castle courtyard. The Earthman instantly shut off his ray, and the others followed his example.

Calling two of his warriors before the instrument board, he instructed them in the use of the projector. He told them that if any of Sel Han's men should attempt to fly up from the courtyard they should be instantly annihilated. And finally he ordered them to watch for him to raise his hand, at which signal they were to blast a hole through the base of the castle wall directly in front of them, then shut off the ray.

These instructions completed, he mounted his gawr, and flinging the bound Ma Gong operator across the front of his saddle, flew to the dock where the main body of his swordsmen waited.

Dismounting, he turned his prisoner over to two guards and called an officer.

"Get me a herald," he commanded.

The officer hurried away, and reappeared in a few moments with a youth who carried a trumpet. Thorne gave him his instructions and he walked toward the gate.

As the Earthman stood looking after him he felt a touch on his arm. Turning, he beheld Neva, who had just come up behind him.

"I cannot find my father," she said. "I've looked for him everywhere. Do you know where he is?"

"I am sorry to say," he replied, "that the Dixtar saw fit to open the castle gates to the enemy. I haven't the slightest idea where he is—probably with his good friend, Sel Han."

She appeared distinctly shocked. "You don't mean—you can't mean . . ."

"That he could have betrayed us? Why not? It seems to run in the family."

She went pale at this, then looked up at him with flashing eyes. "Sheb Takkor Rad," she said, "some day you will regret those words. There are certain things of which you are ignorant, which I hoped you would eventually come to understand. But now—now I don't care. I hate you! I never want to see you again!"

As she flung away from him the notes of the herald's trumpet sounded before the gate.

"The Rad of Takkor," cried the herald, "calls upon Sel Han and his bandits to lay down their arms and march out of the castle. If they fail to comply they will be destroyed utterly, and the castle with them. As a token of surrender they will immediately throw open the gates."

Thorne waited for some time, watching the gates expectantly. They remained closed. He called to the herald. "Continue."

Again the herald sounded his trumpet.

"The Rad of Takkor is inclined to be merciful," he cried, "yet you try him sorely. Behold!"

Thorne raised his hand. A green ray flashed out from the house-top, drilled through the base of the wall, then winked off, leaving a gaping black hole. From within the castle there came the sounds of a mighty tumult—shouts, groans, curses, and the clash of weapons. Suddenly the gates swung open, and there emerged a rabble of yellow warriors, weaponless, thrusting before them two white men whose arms were bound behind them, and carrying on their shoulders the bodies of a dozen more. It was obvious that the Ma Gongi, facing destruction by their own dread weapons, had mutinied to save their lives.

Leaving his gawr in charge of a warrior, Thorne hurried forward. As he drew near the prisoners he recognized the tall, broad-shouldered figure of Sel Han, and the wizened, rat-faced Dixtar. The first corpse, borne by four yellow warriors, was that of Sur Det.

"Surround the Ma Gongi," Thorne shouted to his swordsmen. "Be on the lookout for treachery. And bring me the two white prisoners."

Under the watchful eyes of the Takkor fighting men, the horde of yellow warriors continued to pour from the castle until it was emptied of enemies. Then, at a command from the Earthman, the swordsmen closed in behind them and a small detachment entered the castle to look for stragglers.

"Bring the prisoners and follow me," Thorne ordered.

He led the way to where Miradon Vil stood with Neva, Thaine, Lal Vak and Kov Lutas.

Rendering the imperial salute to the Vil, he said, "Your majesty, I bring you two men who have usurped the throne of your empire, one for a generation, the other for a day. They are your prisoners, to do with as you will. And since the weapons with which Sel Han set out to conquer Mars are in the custody of my swordsmen, you are once more Vil of Xancibar. As for the nest of this would-be world conqueror and his fellow conspirators, which is said to be somewhere on my estate, every prisoner here knows where it is, and I am sure that at least one of them can be persuaded to tell."

"Sheb Takkor Rad," replied Miradon Vil, his voice shaking with emotion, "I find it difficult to express . . ."

He got no further, for at this moment there came a sudden and unexpected interruption. Thorne's first intimation of it was the sound of a sword being whipped from its sheath. He turned in time to see Sel Han, who had managed to slip off his bonds and snatch the sword of the man who guarded him, leap across the space which separated him from the two girls, catch up Thaine, fling her over his shoulder, and dash away.

Drawing his own blade, the Earthman was the first to spring after the fugitive. Only a short way off stood Thorne's gawr, held by a warrior. Sel Han split his head with a blow of the sword and leaped into the saddle.

Still clutching the struggling, kicking Thaine, and holding both her wrists with his left hand, he pulled up on the guiding rod with his right. The great bird-beast lumbered forward and took off, flapping noisily because of the double burden it carried, while Thorne and his companions looked on helplessly, not daring to use their javelins for fear of injuring the girl.

The gawr, obedient to the guiding rod, flew swiftly out over the lake.

CHAPTER 22

Before the sound of Sel Han's derisive laughter died out, Thorne turned and sprinted for the nearest gawr.

"Send five hundred swordsmen after me," he ordered as he sprang into the saddle. "This may lead to an ambush." Then he lifted the guiding rod and was off.

As his bird-beast rose in the air, Thorne saw that Sel Han was already halfway across the lake, and circling toward the northeast, a direction that would carry him over the heart of the marsh and into a terrain altogether strange to the Earthman. A glance behind him showed a horde of his riders coming across the lake. Fearing they might not have marked his course, he raised his baridium torch over his head and flashed it thrice. His signal was answered, almost immediately by three flashes from a rider in the front ranks.

He did not doubt that Sel Han was making for his secret lair, which was believed to be somewhere in Takkor Marsh. But league after league of marshland unrolled beneath them, with the fugitive showing no signs of halting. And gradually, Thorne's swift bird-beast gained on the other. The nearer moon rose, its bright rays accentuating the details of the scene.

Presently, when it seemed that the two moons were about to meet, Thorne noticed a change in the topography of the country ahead. They were nearing a broad, flat-topped mountain with a sloping base of sand and boulders that led to rugged, frowning cliffs.

Sel Han's destination was obviously those frowning cliffs, but as he approached them Thorne noticed that his bird-beast had reached the limit of its endurance.

With its beak almost over the rim, it fell, fluttering weakly and pecking ineffectually at the sheer cliff face with its hooked bill in an effort to save itself. Fortunately there was a shelf of rock only fifty feet below, and on this the creature alighted.

Thorne arrived on that shelf not five seconds later, but Sel Han had already sprung from his saddle, and with Thaine still slung helplessly over his shoulder, was sprinting away along that narrow ledge. Whipping out his sword, the Earthman leaped down and set out in hot pursuit.

Abruptly the ledge curved around a sharp bend in the cliff wall, and for a moment Thorne lost sight of his quarry. Then, as he rounded the bend, he saw them again. They were now in an indentation of the cliff face about an eighth of a mile deep, and the cliff opposite him was honeycombed with baridium-lighted caverns and terraced with ledges that swarmed with Ma Gong workmen. On the top of the cliff above them a troop of mounted yellow warriors sat on guard. This, then, was the hidden nest of the conspirators.

Though not more than five hundred feet separated Sel Han and his followers, he was unable to reach them, for the ledge ended suddenly only a short distance farther on. But if he could not cross to his men, he could call them to him, and this he did.

"Ho, warriors! Your Vildus is beset! To me!"

Instantly there came a chorus of answering cries, and the flapping of their mounts' wings as they took off. Almost at the same moment the vanguard of the Takkor swordsmen rounded the bend in the wall.

Though he had noted all these happenings, Thorne had not slackened his pace; he turned and called to his men.

"Capture those caves," he shouted, pointing across the inlet with his sword, "and everything in them."

Again he turned and dashed forward, then suddenly cried out in consternation. Sel Han and his precious burden had disappeared.

The Takkor swordsmen and the Ma Gong warriors now clashed in midair, but Thorne ran on breathlessly until he reached the very end of the ledge. Then he saw the explanation—a circular doorway hewn in the solid rock at his left.

Fearing an ambush, Thorne stepped warily through that opening. He found himself in an immense cavern, lighted and ventilated by a hole in the roof through which the bright moonlight was streaming. Immediately beneath this hole a narrow wooden bridge crossed a wide chasm which split the floor of the cave from side to side. At the opposite end of the bridge was Sel Han. He had flung Thaine to the floor, and was hacking desperately with his sword at the two slender poles which supported the farther end of the bridge.

Thorne sprang forward, but the wood splintered and the bridge sagged, then fell into the chasm.

Thorne paused on the brink of the chasm. It was fully fifty feet across, and about two hundred feet deep, reaching clear to the smooth walls on both sides.

The Earthman glared at his enemy, who laughed mockingly. Behind him, on a pedestal at the rear of the cave, was a stone colossus with a sardonic grin on its repulsive features, evidently the forgotten god of some vanished race. It almost seemed as if the god had laughed.

"Now if you had a pair of wings . . ." bantered Sel Han, grinning maliciously.

Thorne had no intention of replying, but at this moment he noticed something which made him change his mind. Thaine, lying on the floor behind his enemy, sat up and opened her eyes, looking about her in bewilderment. She still wore her weapons.

"Sel Han, the mighty swordsman," he mocked. "The irresistible Vildus of Mars. I am alone, yet you run away. It must be that you fear me."

"I am too great a man to engage in a common brawl," Sel Han replied. "As soon as my warriors have defeated yours, they will come and cut you into small pieces. Then . . ."

He paused suddenly, having detected a sound behind him. Thaine had sprung to her feet and drawn her sword.

Sel Han still clutched his own weapon. "Put down that sword, you little fool!" he growled. "Do you think you can beat *me*?"

For answer, she extended her blade in a swift lunge that would have stretched an ordinary swordsman on the stone floor. But her abductor was no ordinary swordsman. He parried with a quick riposte.

Thorne realized that Sel Han was thoroughly angry and in deadly earnest. The thrust he had aimed at Thaine's heart was meant to kill!

Suddenly, above the clashing of the blades and panting of the contestants, Thorne heard the sound of footsteps and the clank of weapons behind. Turning, he saw Yirl Du and a dozen Takkor swordsmen.

"The traitors' nest is captured, my lord," announced Yirl Du. Then he saw what was taking place at the other end of the cavern . . . "Why—why!" he stammered.

But on the instant, Thorne had conceived a plan. "Follow me!" he cried. "We can do no good here."

He ran out of the cave, Yirl Du and the warriors at his heels. Their gawrs were perched on the ledge.

The Earthman leaped into a saddle and pulled up the guiding rod. "Come with me, and bring ten men," he told Yirl Du.

Thorne guided the bird-beast up over the rim of the cliff and came down beside the hole in the roof of the cavern. Unhooking the two safety chains from the saddle, he fastened them together. Yirl Du and his ten men alighted around him a moment later.

"Bring me all your safety chains," Thorne ordered.

They brought them, and he swiftly fastened them together, end to end, until he had a chain nearly a hundred feet in length. He hooked one end of this in his belt ring.

"Now let me down that hole and swing me toward the ledge on which they are fighting."

They seized the chain and let him down swiftly. He was directly above the appalling depth of the chasm.

Leaning down over the rim of the hole, Yirl Du set the chain in motion—a pendulum with a slender linked shaft and a human weight.

Nearer and nearer Thorne swung toward his objective, and Sel Han, who had heard the rattle of the chain, broke away from Thaine for a moment, to try to impale the Earthman as he spun helplessly at the end. But Thaine, seeing Thorne's danger, instantly went to his rescue, attacking her abductor so furiously that he was forced to devote all his attention to her.

At last Thorne's feet touched the ledge. The chain slackened, and he reached around to unhook it from his belt ring. This done, he looked up just in time to see a sight that drove him berserk with rage and grief. Two feet of Sel Han's steel were projecting from Thaine's back. With an agonized gasp, Thaine crumpled to the floor.

Thorne sprang furiously to the attack, but rage and grief are poor allies in a contest with swords. The Earthman, fighting his opponent, and little caring what happened to himself, constantly risked desperate lunges which left him dangerously exposed to counter thrusts.

Only when he was bleeding from no less than a score of wounds and felt himself growing weaker did his common sense reassert itself. Resolutely, purposefully, Thorne now began to fence.

Sel Han instantly noticed the change in his antagonist's swordsmanship, and a look of fear came over his flat features. Yet he fought savagely.

Thorne was fencing coolly now, thrusting and parrying with ease and precision. So lightly did he hold the skill of his opponent that on hearing the clank of weapons he took time to glance across the chasm to see who had entered the cave. With a start of surprise he recognized Neva, Miradon Vil, Kov Lutas and Lal Vak. Miradon Vil, he saw, was reaching out for the end of the chain which Yirl Du was swinging toward him. But it was Neva, beside the Vil, who grasped the chain and swung across the chasm.

Thorne was so surprised that he was not quite quick enough in parrying a cut for his head. Sel Han's blade parted his head-strap and bit through into his skull.

He saw a myriad dancing stars, then the blood spurted down into his eyes, half blinding him.

But for all that, he sprang to the attack, forcing his opponent back, back, until he stood on the very edge of the chasm. Again Sel Han tried that headcut which had worked so well before, but this time Thorne saw it coming. He parried, then countered with a sweeping moulinet to the neck—a drawing cut that sheared off the still-grinning head. It fell at his feet, and the body toppled backward into the chasm.

Staggering drunkenly, Thorne kicked the leering head after the body. Then he lurched forward . . .

CHAPTER 23

Thorne opened his eyes slowly, blinked, then opened them again and stared in astonishment. He was looking up at a frescoed ceiling on which was depicted a Martian battle scene—a beleaguered city fighting off the attack of a vast army. Four golden chains depended from the ceiling, supporting the divan on which he lay beneath silken covers of peacock blue embroidered with a design in gold. Swiftly he glanced around, and saw that he was in a luxuriously furnished chamber, lighted by three large circular windows through which the bright sunlight streamed, their crystal segments opened like flower petals to admit the crisp morning air.

Seated in a swinging chair nearby, a man with white hair was poring over the contents of a large scroll.

"Lal Vak!" Thorne exclaimed.

The old scientist turned and smiled. "Ah, you know me at last," he said. He put down his scroll and walked over to the divan.

"Where am I?" Thorne asked him.

"Why, in the palace, of course." He pointed to the silken cover and the embroidered design. "These are the colors, and this the design of the royal family of Xancibar."

"But I don't understand. The last I remember, I was in that cave."

"Precisely. Neva pulled you back from the brink of the chasm. You had lost a deal of blood and fainted in her arms. Yirl Du left guards at the captured nest of the conspirators. Then we picked up five hundred more of your Takkor swordsmen at the castle and flew here. They easily cleared the palace of Sel Han's followers, and Miradon Vil was received and acclaimed by the people with great rejoicing. They were heartily sick of the atrocities of Irintz Tel and the Kamud. But all that took place six days ago. You have been delirious since. Yesterday the royal physician removed the jembal from your wounds and pronounced them healed. And last night you fell into a deep, healthful sleep which he believed would restore you."

Thorne raised his hand, and felt the scar on his head reflectively. Again he saw the horror of the struggle in the cave . . . "Poor Thaine," he murmured.

"But Thaine is better," said Lal Vak. "The physician says she can be up and around in a day or two."

"What! I thought her dead."

"The wound was high—painful, but not dangerous."

Thorne threw back the covers and swung his legs over the edge of the bed. His head reeled dizzily.

"Where are you going?"

"To Thaine," Thorne replied.

"But you can't get up yet."

"Can't I?"

Thorne stood erect, swaying uncertainly. His legs were very weak and he felt light-headed. A jar of pulcho and several cups stood on a near-by stand. Lal Vak filled a cup and handed it to him. He drank it off at a gulp and called for another. Then he staggered to the bath box, declining the assistance of his white-haired friend. Stepping out of his sleeping garment, he entered, closed the door, and trod on the plate. A few moments later he emerged, dripping and brushing the water from his eyes. When he opened them he saw a familiar figure standing before him with two great wisps of dry moss.

"Vorz!" he exclaimed.

"The same, my lord," replied the little orderly, and proceeded to give him a brisk rub-down. "His majesty granted me leave to serve you, and I trust you will not send me away."

"Not I," Thorne replied. "If his majesty permits, I'll take you back to Takkor with me."

"Thank you, my lord."

Vorz had laid out his clothing and weapons for him, and these he now proceeded to don. There was a magnificent cloak of orange trimmed with black, the colors of nobility. Then there was the Takkor medallion to hang about his neck. And a jeweled sword and dagger with Takkor serpent hilts.

"Do I look all right to go calling on a lady, Vorz?" he asked.

"Magnificent, my lord," was the reply. And Thorne thought of the last time Vorz had groomed him, the night of Irintz Tel's reception, when he and Neva had plighted their troth and she, when they were discovered, had condemned him to the baridium mines. But now there was another picture to add which puzzled and somehow comforted him. It was the memory of Neva swinging across the chasm at the risk of her own life and drawing him back from the brink just in time to save him.

"Come," he said, taking the arm of his old friend. "Let us find the apartment of Thaine."

They strode through the hallways in silence for a time. Then Thorne thought of Irintz Tel. "What has become of the Dixtar?"

"I'll show you," replied Lal Vak.

Presently they came to a door; the scientist drew a large key from his belt, unlocked the door, and threw it open.

"Enter," he invited.

Thorne stepped inside and recognized the Hall of Heads. There were the shelves, reaching to the ceiling, with their thousands of grisly relics. Then he saw that a pedestal had been set up in the center of the hall. On the pedestal was a jar; a pair of small, beady eyes, glazed with the film of death, looked out at him sightlessly from a wizened, ratlike face.

"Irintz Tel!" he exclaimed. "Well I can't say that I blame Miradon Vil."

113

"You wrong his majesty," said Lal Vak. "The Vil had nothing to do with this. In fact he had granted the Dixtar full pardon, and bestowed on him a magnificent estate on the Zeelan Canal. But the next day Irintz Tel disappeared. An anonymous note was received that night suggesting that we look here. And we found this. We think it was the work of relatives of some of his victims. But no search is being conducted. The thing is done, and cannot be remedied. After all, they were certainly justified."

They quitted that place of horrors and came to the apartment of Thaine. A guard saluted and admitted them; a slave girl bade them be seated while she went in to announce them to her mistress.

"I'll wait here for you," said Lal Vak, "since I have already paid my respects to the young lady this morning."

Thorne went in alone. On a luxurious divan beneath fluffy blue silk coverlets lay Thaine.

"Hahr Ree Thorne!" she cried a trifle faintly, and held up both arms to him. He bent, and the arms went around his neck—drew his face to hers. Their lips met.

"You should not be up," she said reprovingly, "for you were worse injured than I."

"My scratches have healed," he laughed, "and now I'm ready to leave—to go back to Takkor. I don't care for cities—or palaces."

"Nor I," she told him. "This is such a big lonesome place. Already I am homesick for the marsh—for the hunting and fishing, and the blazing log fires in the evenings."

It suddenly occurred to Thorne that, since he had put Neva forever from his mind, life would be far more worth the living with Thaine by his side.

"Thaine," he said, "do you remember that day in your father's cabin when you tried a certain experiment?"

She smiled up at him. "How could I forget?"

"And you said you must have time to think."

"Since then I have thought—much. I was so inexperienced—I thought love was a thing which might be cultivated, little knowing that it is a flower which springs up spontaneously in the heart."

"Thaine! You can't mean that at last . . ."

"Yes, Hahr Ree Thorne. At last I have found true love. It came to me so unexpectedly, when I met Kov Lutas, that it left me weak and breathless."

"Kov Lutas!"

"Why, yes. We are to be wed as soon as I am well. Hadn't you heard?"

Thorne achieved a smile, but in his heart there was a feeling of emptiness—of desolation. He forced his lips to say the conventional things, to wish her joy and to proclaim Kov Lutas the luckiest man on Mars. But to himself he thought: *First Sylvia, then Neva, and now Thaine! It is my destiny to be alone and loveless.*

Rising, he said: "I must go now and prepare for my journey. Farewell, and Deza grant you much happiness."

Once outside her door, however, he could dissemble no longer. Lal Vak remarked his woebegone expression.

"Why so sad?" he asked. "I trust you found the lady well."

"Perfectly," Thorne replied. Then added: "Old friend, I'm a fool ever to have anything to do with women. From now on, I'm through, and I mean it."

"Why, what's this?" asked the scientist. "Do you fall in love with every woman you meet?"

"Well, not exactly that. But since Neva betrayed me . . ."

"Betrayed you! What talk is this? Why she has twice saved your life! What are you talking about, boy?"

"You should know as well as I," Thorne said bitterly. "Was it not she who sent me to the baridium mines?"

Lal Vak looked at him quizzically for the moment. "You are a greater fool than I thought, my boy. She sent you to the baridium mines to save you from the headsman. And who do you think it was who aided you to escape from the mines? There were only three people in Xancibar with the power to do so. The other two were Irintz Tel and Sel Han. Do you think *they* did it?"

"Why I thought it was you."

"I had a small part," Lal Vak admitted, "but it was she who engineered everything—who pulled the strings and moved the officials in high places, so the thing could be accomplished. You should have seen her, tearful and apprehensive that next day, as she connived with Kov Lutas and me to win your freedom. And after the thing had been done, she was beside herself with worry for fear you would be captured. Every day she besought me to try to obtain news of you. You should know, also, that the tales of her heartless flirtations were utterly false, invented by Sel Han and spread by his henchmen to keep off powerful rivals. She was no more a murderous siren than our little Thaine. That I can attest, and I have known her all her life."

Thorne was stunned. "I have done her a great wrong, old friend," he said, "and not only in my heart. I openly cut her when she held out her arms to me that night in Takkor Castle. I have lost the only woman I ever really loved through my own lack of faith."

"She saved your life in the cave at the risk of her own," Lal Vak reminded him. "Is that the act of one who has ceased to care?"

"I don't know," groaned Thorne. "The more I see of women the less I understand them."

"At least, you should call on her and apologize."

"That I will do. Let us go to her apartment."

As they approached the door of Neva's apartment, two guards saluted smartly and stood aside for them to enter. In the reception room a slave girl met them. "Tell your mistress Sheb Takkor is calling," Thorne told her.

The slave girl returned almost immediately. "My mistress is not receiving callers, my lord," she said.

Thorne turned to Lal Vak. "You see, I was right," he said. "But it is no more than I deserve for my little faith. Come. Let us go back to my apartment. I must prepare for my journey."

CHAPTER 24

Back in his apartment with Lal Vak, Thorne notified Vorz that they were leaving. Then he went to the writing board, spread a scroll, and composed a letter. Then he rolled it, placed it in a wooden tube, and handed it to Lal Vak.

"Give this to Neva after I am gone," he said, "and I shall be grateful to you. I have apologized for my boorish conduct and thanked her for having twice saved my life—a life that has become empty and purposeless without her. But it is, as you have said, the least I can do, and unfortunately, the most I can do, as well."

Lal Vak thrust the cylinder under his belt. "I'll be glad to deliver this for you," he said. "Now I'll go out and arrange for your transportation."

Presently he returned. "A flying machine awaits you on the roof," he said, "and his majesty is ready to receive you."

Thorne emptied his pulcho cup and arose. The scientist conducted him to a reception room where Miradon Vil, resplendent in his royal cloak of peacock blue trimmed with gold, was standing on the dais before the throne addressing a number of his nobles. But when the Rad of Takkor was announced, he dismissed them all and stepped down to receive his guest.

"My boy," he said, "I am happy to see you well, and with your memory and reason restored."

"And I," replied Thorne, "am equally happy to see your majesty restored to the throne of your ancestors; but no happier, I am sure, than every citizen, high and low, in Xancibar."

"Some time ago," said Miradon, "I rendered you the empty thanks of a deposed Vil. Today I am in a position to show my gratitude more tangibly and practically. First, I free you and Takkor from all allegiance to Xancibar. This makes you the supreme ruler of the raddek, and the collector and dispenser of all Takkor revenues.

"Second, I have conferred with the Vils of the other great powers of Mars, and we have decided that you shall be the arbiter of our destinies. You captured the weapons and the laboratory with which Sel Han sought to conquer Mars. In unscrupulous hands they could do much harm. But we have faith in you. We want you to keep them, to protect us against any other ambitious plotters who may arise, so that we may fight our wars and settle our differences with the weapons of honor and chivalry we have always used. So, in effect, we make you the custodian of our liberty."

From a taboret which stood beside the dais, he took a golden medal, set with sparkling jewels and hung on a heavy golden chain. "This commemorates our resolution, and is the badge of your high office."

Inscribed on the medal Thorne read:

SHEB TAKKOR
Supreme Arbiter of Destiny
and
Custodian of Liberty
by the will of the
Associated Vilets
of Mars

The Vil snapped the chain around Thorne's neck, so the new medal flashed and scintillated on his chest just above the Takkor medallion.

"I am overwhelmed, your majesty," said Thorne. "The nations of Mars have placed too high a value on my poor services."

Miradon smiled and stroked his silky golden beard. "There is but one more thing, and I will give you leave to go."

He raised his hand, and a flourish of trumpets sounded from the doorway. Two heralds entered, trumpets resting on hips. Behind them came six pages, carrying a gold-embroidered cloak of peacock blue like that worn by the Vil. Following the pages was another, bearing a jar of pulcho and a gem-encrusted golden cup.

The heralds separated, and stood, one at each side of the dais. The pages held the cloak spread before the Vil.

"Permit me," said Miradon, unfastening Thorne's head straps and removing his cloak of orange and black. He handed the cloak to a slave, and taking the one which the pages had brought, fastened its jeweled straps about Thorne's head. Then the last page came up with the pulcho and the cup.

Filling the cup, the Vil drank half its contents, then passed it to Thorne. "Drink," he commanded.

Thorne drained the cup and returned it to the tray.

The Vil raised both hands before his face. "I shield my eyes to the Zovil of Xancibar," he said.

Thorne raised his hands and responded to the salutation.

"That is all," said Miradon. "And now, since you insist on leaving us so soon, Lal Vak will conduct you to the roof. I will be there to see you off in a few moments."

In the company of the scientist Thorne left the presence, and climbed the stairs toward the roof.

"Tell me something, Lal Vak," said Thorne. "What is the significance of this cloak? And what is a zovil?"

"A zovil," replied the scientist, "is a vil's son, just as a zorad is a rad's son. The cloak, and the ceremony that went with it, made you a prince of the imperial house of Xancibar."

"I seem to have gotten almost everything on this planet but the one I want the most," said Thorne morosely.

"I presume that you refer to Neva," said Lal Vak. "Well, don't consider her totally lost to you, yet. Women have been known to change their minds, you know."

On the roof of the palace a great metal flying machine stood waiting. Standing around it was a group of the most exalted nobles and officials of Xancibar.

A moment later the leonine head of Miradon Vil appeared above the top of the stairway. As he stepped out on the roof the courtiers again rendered the imperial salute. He walked up to Thorne and placed his huge hands on his shoulders.

"Farewell, my son," he said, "and take good care of that which I have entrusted to you."

As he spoke, it seemed to Thorne that his voice broke slightly, and there was a suspicion of tears in his eyes.

"Farewell, your majesty," Thorne replied.

The warrior went up to the forward cab with Vorz and the pilot, and closed the door after him. Thorne turned to select a seat. Then he gasped in amazement.

Seated near a window was Neva, clad in a most becoming costume of peacock blue, embroidered with gold. She smiled up at Thorne as he hurried to her side and bent over her. "You!" he exclaimed. "I can't believe my eyes!"

"Lal Vak brought me your note," she said. "After I had read it I decided to forgive you."

"But—but, how came you here, and wearing the colors of royalty?"

"Since I am the only daughter of Miradon Vil, there is no one who has a better right to these colors."

"But what of Thaine?"

"Thaine," replied Neva, "is the daughter of Irintz Tel. Miradon Vil—my father—when he went into exile, was determined to insure my safety, and to give me the advantages which were rightfully mine. So he exchanged me for Thaine when we were babies. Thaine doesn't know, yet, and I only learned the truth five days ago."

Looking at her, Thorne decided that he must have been blind not to realize the resemblance between the fair-haired Vil and this girl before.

"Then—then his majesty, your father, knows you have come with me?"

"Of course. Why else should he have performed the ceremony that made you Zovil of Xancibar?"

"I'm sure I don't know."

"Because, stupid, he could only make you a prince of his house by making you my husband. There is no other way."

Full realization suddenly came to him. He caught her in his arms, sought and found her yielding lips. "Neva, beloved!" he murmured. "Are you really my wife?"

"Unto death, Deza help you!" she replied archly.

But there was a starry light in her glorious eyes which he could not fail to understand.

www.ingramcontent.com/pod-product-compliance
Lightning Source LLC
Chambersburg PA
CBHW031842170626
46807CB00004B/1574